THE PILGRIM OF HATE

THE PILGRIM
OF HATE

*The Tenth Chronicle
of Brother Cadfael*

Ellis Peters

Thorndike Press
Thorndike, Maine USA

This Large Print edition is published by Thorndike Press, USA.

Published in 1999 in the U.S. by arrangement with Deborah Owen Limited.

U.S. Softcover ISBN 0–7862–1945–9 (General Series Edition)

The text of this Large Print edition is unabridged.
Other aspects of the book may vary from the original edition.

Set in 16 pt. New Times Roman.

Printed in Great Britain on acid-free paper.

Library of Congress Cataloging-in-Publication Data

Peters, Ellis, 1913–
    The pilgrim of hate : the tenth chronicle of Brother Cadfael / Ellis Peters.
      p.   cm.
    ISBN 0–7862–1945–9 (lg. print : sc : alk. paper)
    1. Cadfael, Brother (Fictitious character) Fiction.   2. Great Britain—History—Stephen, 1135–1154 Fiction.
    3. Herbalists—England—Shrewsbury Fiction.   4. Monks—England—Shrewsbury Fiction.   5. Shrewsbury (England) Fiction.
    6. Large type books.   I. Title.
    [PR6031.A49P5   1999]
    823'.912—dc21   99–14891

CHAPTER ONE

They were together in Brother Cadfael's hut in the herbarium, in the afternoon of the twenty-fifth day of May, and the talk was of high matters of state, of kings and empresses, and the unbalanced fortunes that plagued the irreconcilable contenders for thrones.

'Well, the lady is not crowned yet!' said Hugh Beringar, almost as firmly as if he saw a way of preventing it.

'She is not even in London yet,' agreed Cadfael, stirring carefully round the pot embedded in the coals of his brazier, to keep the brew from boiling up against the sides and burning. 'She cannot well be crowned until they let her in to Westminster. Which it seems, from all I gather, they are in no hurry to do.'

'Where the sun shines,' said Hugh ruefully, 'there whoever's felt the cold will gather. My cause, old friend, is out of the sun. When Henry of Blois shifts, all men shift with him, like starvelings huddled in one bed. He heaves the coverlet, and they go with him, clinging by the hems.'

'Not all,' objected Cadfael, briefly smiling as he stirred. 'Not you. Do you think you are the only one?'

'God forbid!' said Hugh, and suddenly laughed, shaking off his gloom. He came back

1

from the open doorway, where the pure light spread a soft golden sheen over the bushes and beds of the herb-garden and the moist noon air drew up a heady languor of spiced and drunken odours, and plumped his slender person down again on the bench against the timber wall, spreading his booted feet on the earth floor. A small man in one sense only, and even so trimly made. His modest stature and light weight had deceived many a man to his undoing. The sunshine from without, fretted by the breeze that swayed the bushes, was reflected from one of Cadfael's great glass flagons to illuminate by flashing glimpses a lean, tanned face, clean shaven, with a quirky mouth, and agile black eyebrows that could twist upward sceptically into cropped black hair. A face at once eloquent and inscrutable. Brother Cadfael was one of the few who knew how to read it. Doubtful if even Hugh's wife Aline understood him better. Cadfael was in his sixty-second year, and Hugh still a year or two short of thirty but, meeting thus in easy companionship in Cadfael's workshop among the herbs, they felt themselves contemporaries.

'No,' said Hugh, eyeing circumstances narrowly, and taking some cautious comfort, 'not all. There are a few of us yet, and not so badly placed to hold on to what we have. There's the queen in Kent with her army.

Robert of Gloucester is not going to turn his back to come hunting us here while she hangs on the southern fringes of London. And with the Welsh of Gwynedd keeping our backs against the earl of Chester, we can hold this shire for King Stephen and wait out the time. Luck that turned once can turn again. And the empress is not queen of England yet.'

But for all that, thought Cadfael, mutely stirring his brew for Brother Aylwin's scouring calves, it began to look as though she very soon would be. Three years of civil war between cousins fighting for the sovereignty of England had done nothing to reconcile the factions, but much to sicken the general populace with insecurity, rapine and killing. The craftsman in the town, the cottar in the village, the serf on the demesne, would be only too glad of any monarch who could guarantee him a quiet and orderly country in which to carry on his modest business. But to a man like Hugh it was no such indifferent matter. He was King Stephen's liege man, and now King Stephen's sheriff of Shropshire, sworn to hold the shire for his cause. And his king was a prisoner in Bristol castle since the lost battle of Lincoln. A single February day of this year had seen a total reversal of the fortunes of the two claimants to the throne. The Empress Maud was up in the clouds, and Stephen, crowned and anointed though he might be, was down in the midden, close-bound and close-guarded, and his brother Henry of Blois, bishop of Winchester and papal legate, far the most influential of the magnates and hitherto his brother's supporter, had found himself in a dilemma. He could either be a hero, and adhere loudly and firmly to his allegiance, thus incurring the formidable animosity of a lady who was in the ascendant and could be dangerous, or trim his sails and accommodate himself to the reverses of fortune by coming over to her side. Discreetly, of course, and with well-prepared arguments to render his about-face respectable. It was just possible, thought Cadfael, willing to do justice even to bishops, that Henry also had the cause of order and peace genuinely at heart, and was willing to back whichever contender could restore them.

'What frets me,' said Hugh restlessly, 'is that I can get no reliable news. Rumours enough and more than enough, every new one laying the last one dead, but nothing a man can grasp and put his trust in. I shall be main glad when Abbot Radulfus comes home.'

'So will every brother in this house,' agreed Cadfael fervently. 'Barring Jerome, perhaps, he's in high feather when Prior Robert is left in charge, and a fine time he's had of it all these weeks since the abbot was summoned to Winchester. But Robert's rule is less favoured by the rest of us, I can tell you.'

'How long is it he's been away now?' pondered Hugh. 'Seven or eight weeks! The legate's keeping his court well stocked with mitres all this time. Maintaining his own state no doubt gives him some aid in confronting hers. Not a man to let his dignity bow to princes, Henry, and he needs all the weight he can get at his back.'

'He's letting some of his cloth disperse now, however,' said Cadfael. 'By that token, he may have got a kind of settlement. Or he may be deceived into thinking he has. Father Abbot sent word from Reading. In a week he should be here. You'll hardly find a better witness.'

Bishop Henry had taken good care to keep the direction of events in his own hands. Calling all the prelates and mitred abbots to Winchester early in April, and firmly declaring the gathering a legatine council, no mere church assembly, had ensured his supremacy at the subsequent discussions, giving him precedence over Archbishop Theobald of Canterbury, who in purely English church matters was his superior. Just as well, perhaps. Cadfael doubted if Theobald had greatly minded being outflanked. In the circumstances a quiet, timorous man might be only too glad to lurk peaceably in the shadows, and let the legate bear the heat of the sun.

'I know it. Once let me hear his account of what's gone forward, down there in the south, and I can make my own dispositions. We're remote enough here, and the queen, God keep her, has gathered a very fair array, now she has the Flemings who escaped from Lincoln to add to her force. She'll move heaven and earth to get Stephen out of hold, by whatever means, fair or foul. She is,' said Hugh with conviction, 'a better soldier than her lord. Not a better fighter in the field—God knows you'd need to search Europe through to find such a one, I saw him at Lincoln—a marvel! But a better general, that she *is*. She holds to her purpose, where he tires and goes off after another quarry. They tell me, and I believe it, she's drawing her cordon closer and closer to London, south of the river. The nearer her rival comes to Westminster, the tighter that noose will be drawn.'

'And is it certain the Londoners have agreed to let the empress in? We hear they came late to the council, and made a faint plea for Stephen before they let themselves be tamed. It takes a very stout heart, I suppose, to stand up to Henry of Winchester face to face, and deny him,' allowed Cadfael, sighing.

'They've agreed to admit her, which is as good as acknowledging her. But they're arguing terms for her entry, as I heard it, and every delay is worth gold to me and to Stephen. If only,' said Hugh, the dancing light suddenly sharpening every line of his intent and eloquent face, 'if only I could get a good man into Bristol! There are ways into castles, even into the dungeons. Two or three good, secret men might do it. A fistful of gold to a

6

malcontent gaoler . . . Kings have been fetched off before now, even out of chains, and he's not chained. She has not gone so far, not yet. Cadfael, I dream! My work is here, and I am but barely equal to it. I have no means of carrying off Bristol, too.'

'Once loosed,' said Cadfael, 'your king is going to need this shire ready to his hand.'

He turned from the brazier, hoisting aside the pot and laying it to cool on a slab of stone he kept for the purpose. His back creaked a little as he straightened it. In small ways he was feeling his years, but once erect he was spry enough.

'I'm done here for this while,' he said, brushing his hands together to get rid of the hollow worn by the ladle. 'Come into the daylight, and see the flowers we're bringing on for the festival of Saint Winifred. Father Abbot will be home in good time to preside over her reception from Saint Giles. And we shall have a houseful of pilgrims to care for.'

*   *   *

They had brought the reliquary of the Welsh saint four years previously from Gwytherin, where she lay buried, and installed it on the altar of the church at the hospital of Saint Giles, at the very edge of Shrewsbury's Foregate suburb, where the sick, the infected, the deformed, the lepers, who might not

7

venture within the walls, were housed and cared for. And thence they had borne her casket in splendour to her altar in the abbey church, to be an ornament and a wonder, a means of healing and blessing to all who came reverently and in need. This year they had undertaken to repeat that last journey, to bring her from Saint Giles in procession, and open her altar to all who came with prayers and offerings. Every year she had drawn many pilgrims. This year they would be legion.

'A man might wonder,' said Hugh, standing spread-footed among the flower beds just beginning to burn from the soft, shy colours of spring into the blaze of summer, 'whether you were not rather preparing for a bridal.'

Hedges of hazel and may-blossom shed silver petals and dangled pale, silver-green catkins round the enclosure where they stood, cowslips were rearing in the grass of the meadow beyond, and irises were in tight, thrusting bud. Even the roses showed a harvest of buds, erect and ready to break and display the first colour. In the walled shelter of Cadfael's herb-garden there were fat globes of peonies, too, just cracking their green sheaths. Cadfael had medicinal uses for the seeds, and Brother Petrus, the abbot's cook, used them as spices in the kitchen.

'A man might not be so far out, at that,' said Cadfael, viewing the fruits of his labours complacently. 'A perpetual and pure bridal.

This Welsh girl was virgin until the day of her death.'

'And you have married her off since?'

It was idly said, in revulsion from pondering matters of state. In such a garden a man could believe in peace, fruitfulness and amity. But it encountered suddenly so profound and pregnant a silence that Hugh pricked up his ears, and turned his head almost stealthily to study his friend, even before the unguarded answer came. Unguarded either from absence of mind, or of design, there was no telling.

'Not wedded,' said Cadfael, 'but certainly bedded. With a good man, too, and her honest champion. He deserved his reward.'

Hugh raised quizzical brows, and cast a glance over his shoulder towards the long roof of the great abbey church, where reputedly the lady in question slept in a sealed reliquary on her own altar. An elegant coffin just long enough to contain a small and holy Welshwoman, with the neat, compact bones of her race.

'Hardly room within there for two,' he said mildly.

'Not two of our gross make, no, not there. There was space enough where we put them.' He knew he was listened to, now, and heard with sharp intelligence, if not yet understood.

'Are you telling me,' wondered Hugh no less mildly, 'that she is *not* there in that elaborate shrine of yours, where everyone else *knows* she is?'

'Can I tell? Many a time I've wished it could be possible to be in two places at once. A thing too hard for me, but for a saint, perhaps, possible? Three nights and three days she was in there, that I do know. She may well have left a morsel of her holiness within—if only by way of thanks to us who took her out again, and put her back where I still, and always shall, believe she wished to be. But for all that,' owned Cadfael, shaking his head, 'there's a trailing fringe of doubt that nags at me. How if I read her wrong?'

'Then your only resort is confession and penance,' said Hugh lightly.

'Not until Brother Mark is full-fledged a priest!' Young Mark was gone from his mother-house and from his flock at Saint Giles, gone to the household of the bishop of Lichfield, with Leoric Aspley's endowment to see him through his studies, and the goal of all his longings shining distant and clear before him, the priesthood for which God had designed him. 'I'm saving for him,' said Cadfael, 'all those sins I feel, perhaps mistakenly, to be no sins. He was my right hand and a piece of my heart for three years, and knows me better than any man living. Barring, it may be, yourself?' he added, and slanted a guileless glance at his friend. 'He will know the truth of me, and by his judgement and for his absolution I'll embrace any

10

penance. You might deliver the judgement, Hugh, but you cannot deliver the absolution.'

'Nor the penance, neither,' said Hugh, and laughed freely. 'So tell it to me, and go free without penalty.'

The idea of confiding was unexpectedly pleasing and acceptable. 'It's a long story,' [See *A Morbid Taste for Bones*.] said Cadfael warningly.

'Then now's your time, for whatever I can do here is done, nothing is asked of me but watchfulness and patience, and why should I wait unentertained if there's a good story to be heard? And you are at leisure until Vespers. You may even get merit,' said Hugh, composing his face into priestly solemnity, 'by unburdening your soul to the secular arm. And I can be secret,' he said, 'as any confessional.'

'Wait, then,' said Cadfael, 'while I fetch a draught of that maturing wine, and come within to the bench under the north wall, where the afternoon sun falls. We may as well be at ease while I talk.'

*   *   *

'It was a year or so before I knew you,' said Cadfael, bracing his back comfortably against the warmed, stony roughness of the herb-garden wall. 'We were without a tame saint to our house, and somewhat envious of Wenlock, where the Cluny community had discovered

11

their Saxon foundress Milburga, and were making great play with her. And we had certain signs that sent off an ailing brother of ours into Wales, to bathe at Holywell, where this girl Winifred died her first death, and brought forth her healing spring. There was her own patron, Saint Beuno, ready and able to bring her back to life, but the spring remained, and did wonders. So it came to Prior Robert that the lady could be persuaded to leave Gwytherin, where she died her second death and was buried, and come and bring her glory to us here in Shrewsbury. I was one of the party he took with him to deal with the parish there, and bring them to give up the saint's bones.'

'All of which,' said Hugh, warmed and attentive beside him, 'I know very well, since all men here know it.'

'Surely! But you do not know to the end what followed. There was one Welsh lord in Gwytherin who would not suffer the girl to be disturbed, and would not be persuaded or bribed or threatened into letting her go. And he died, Hugh—murdered. By one of us, a brother who came from high rank, and had his eyes already set on a mitre. And when we came near to accusing him, it was his life or a better. There were certain young people of that place put in peril by him, the dead lord's daughter and her lover. The boy lashed out in anger, with good reason, seeing his girl

12

wounded and bleeding. He was stronger than he knew. The murderer's neck was broken.'

'How many knew of this?' asked Hugh, his eyes narrowed thoughtfully upon the glossy-leaved rose-bushes.

'When it befell, only the lovers, the dead man and I. And Saint Winifred, who had been raised from her grave and laid in that casket of which you and all men know. *She* knew. She was there. From the moment I raised her,' said Cadfael, 'and by God, it was I who took her from the soil, and I who restored her—and still that makes me glad—from the moment I uncovered those slender bones, I felt in mine they wished only to be left in peace. It was so little and so wild and quiet a graveyard there, with the small church long out of use, meadow flowers growing over all, and the mounds so modest and green. And Welsh soil! The girl was Welsh, like me, her church was of the old persuasion, what did she know of this alien English shire? And I had those young things to keep. Who would have taken their word or mine against all the force of the church? They would have closed their ranks to bury the scandal, and bury the boy with it, and he guilty of nothing but defending his dear. So I took measures.'

Hugh's mobile lips twitched. 'Now indeed you amaze me! And what measures were those? With a dead brother to account for, and Prior Robert to keep sweet . . .'

'Ah, well, Robert is a simpler soul than he supposes, and then I had a good deal of help from the dead brother himself. He'd been busy building himself such a reputation for sanctity, delivering messages from the saint herself—it was he told us she was offering the grave she'd left to the murdered man—and going into trance-sleeps, and praying to leave this world and be taken into bliss living . . . So we did him that small favour. He'd been keeping a solitary night-watch in the old church, and in the morning when it ended, there were his habit and sandals fallen together at his prayer-stool, and the body of him lifted clean out of them, in sweet odours and a shower of may-blossom. That was how he claimed the saint had already visited him, why should not Robert recall it and believe? Certainly he was gone. Why look for him? Would a modest brother of our house be running through the Welsh woods mother-naked?'

'Are you telling me,' asked Hugh cautiously, 'That what you have there in the reliquary is *not* . . . Then the casket had not yet been sealed?' His eyebrows were tangling with his black forelock, but his voice was soft and unsurprised.

'Well . . .' Cadfael twitched his blunt brown nose bashfully between finger and thumb. 'Sealed it was, but there are ways of dealing with seals that leave them unblemished. It's one of the more dubious of my remembered

14

skills, but for all that I was glad of it then.'

'And you put the lady back in the place that was hers, along with her champion?'

'He was a decent, good man, and had spoken up for her nobly. She would not grudge him house-room. I have always thought,' confided Cadfael, 'that she was not displeased with us. She has shown her power in Gwytherin since that time, by many miracles, so I cannot believe she is angry. But what a little troubles me is that she has not so far chosen to favour us with any great mark of her patronage here, to keep Robert happy, and set my mind at rest. Oh, a few little things, but nothing of unmistakable note. How if I have displeased her, after all? Well for me, who *know* what we have within there on the altar—and *mea culpa* if I did wrongly! But what of the innocents who do *not* know, and come in good faith, hoping for grace from her? What if I have been the means of their deprivation and loss?'

'I see,' said Hugh with sympathy, 'that Brother Mark had better make haste through the degrees of ordination, and come quickly to lift the load from you. Unless,' he added with a flashing sidelong smile, 'Saint Winifred takes pity on you first, and sends you a sign.'

'I still do not see,' mused Cadfael, 'what else I could have done. It was an ending that satisfied everyone, both here and there. The children were free to marry and be happy, the

15

village still had its saint, and she had her own people round her. Robert had what he had gone to find—or thought he had, which is the same thing. And Shrewsbury abbey has its festival, with every hope of a full guest-hall, and glory and gain in good measure. If she would but just cast an indulgent look this way, and wink her eye, to let me know I understood her aright.'

'And you've never said word of this to anyone?'

'Never a word. But the whole village of Gwytherin knows it,' admitted Cadfael with a remembering grin. 'No one told, no one had to tell, but they knew. There wasn't a man missing when we took up the reliquary and set out for home. They helped to carry it, whipped together a little chariot to bear it. Robert thought he had them nicely tamed, even those who'd been most reluctant from the first. It was a great joy to him. A simple soul at bottom! It would be great pity to undo him now, when he's busy writing his book about the saint's life, and how he brought her to Shrewsbury.'

'I would not have the heart to put him to such distress,' said Hugh. 'Least said, best for all. Thanks be to God, I have nothing to do with canon law, the common law of a land almost without law costs me enough pains.' No need to say that Cadfael could be sure of his secrecy, that was taken for granted on both sides. 'Well, you speak the lady's own tongue, no doubt she understood you well enough, with or without words. Who knows? When this festival of yours takes place—the twenty-second day of June, you say?—she may take pity on you, and send you a great miracle to set your mind at rest.'

*   *   *

And so she might, thought Cadfael an hour later, on his way to obey the summons of the Vesper bell. Not that he had deserved so signal an honour, but there surely must be one somewhere among the unceasing stream of pilgrims who did deserve it, and could not with justice be rejected. He would be perfectly and humbly and cheerfully content with that. What if she was eighty miles or so away, in what was left of her body? It had been a miraculous body in this life, once brutally dead and raised alive again, what limits of time or space could be set about such a being? If it so pleased her she could be both quiet and content in her grave with Rhisiart, lulled by bird-song in the hawthorn trees, and here attentive and incorporeal, a little flame of spirit in the coffin of unworthy Columbanus, who had killed not for her exaltation but for his own.

Brother Cadfael went to Vespers curiously relieved at having confided to his friend a secret from before the time when they had first

17

known each other, in the beginning as potential antagonists stepping subtly to outwit each other, then discovering how much they had in common, the old man—alone with himself Cadfael admitted to being somewhat over the peak of a man's prime—and the young one, just setting out, exceedingly well-equipped in shrewdness and wit, to build his fortune and win his wife. And both he had done, for he was now undisputed sheriff of Shropshire, if under a powerless and captive king, and up there in the town, near St Mary's church, his wife and his year-old son made a nest for his private happiness when he shut the door on his public burdens.

Cadfael thought of his godson, the sturdy imp who already clutched his way lustily round the rooms of Hugh's town house, climbed unaided into a godfather's lap, and began to utter human sounds of approval, enquiry, indignation and affection. Every man asks of heaven a son. Hugh had his, as promising a sprig as ever budded from the stem. So, by proxy, had Cadfael, a son in God.

There was, after all, a great deal of human happiness in the world, even a world so torn and mangled with conflict, cruelty and greed. So it had always been, and always would be. And so be it, provided the indomitable spark of joy never went out.

* * *

In the refectory, after supper and grace, in the grateful warmth and lingering light of the end of May, when they were shuffling their benches to rise from table, Prior Robert Pennant rose first in his place, levering erect his more than six feet of lean, austere prelate, silver-tonsured and ivory-featured.

'Brothers, I have received a further message from Father Abbot. He has reached Warwick on his way home to us, and hopes to be with us by the fourth day of June or earlier. He bids us be diligent in making proper preparation for the celebration of Saint Winifred's translation, our most gracious patroness.' Perhaps the abbot had so instructed, in duty bound, but it was Robert himself who laid such stress on it, viewing himself, as he did, as the patron of their patroness. His large patrician eye swept round the refectory tables, settling upon those heads most deeply committed. 'Brother Anselm, you have the music already in hand?'

Brother Anselm the precentor, whose mind seldom left its neums and instruments for many seconds together, looked up vaguely, awoke to the question, and stared, wide-eyed. 'The entire order of procession and office is ready,' he said, in amiable surprise that anyone should feel it necessary to ask.

'And Brother Denis, you have made all the preparations necessary for stocking your halls to feed great numbers? For we shall surely need every cot and every dish we can muster.'

Brother Denis the hospitaller, accustomed to outer panics and secure ruler of his own domain, testified calmly that he had made the fullest provision he considered needful, and further, that he had reserves laid by to tap at need.

'There will also be many sick persons to be tended, for that reason they come.'

Brother Edmund the infirmarer, not waiting to be named, said crisply that he had taken into account the probable need, and was prepared for the demands that might be made on his beds and medicines. He mentioned also, being on his feet, that Brother Cadfael had already provided stocks of all the remedies most likely to be wanted, and stood ready to meet any other needs that should arise.

'That is well,' said Prior Robert. 'Now, Father Abbot has yet a special request to make until he comes. He asks that prayers be made at every High Mass for the repose of the soul of a good man, treacherously slain in Winchester as he strove to keep the peace and reconcile faction with faction, in Christian duty.'

For a moment it seemed to Brother Cadfael, and perhaps to most of the others present, that the death of one man, far away in the south, hardly rated so solemn a mention and so signal a mark of respect, in a country where deaths had been commonplace for so long, from the field of Lincoln strewn with bodies to the sack of Worcester with its streets running blood, from the widespread baronial slaughters by disaffected earls to the sordid village banditries where law had broken down. Then he looked at it again, and with the abbot's measuring eyes. Here was a good man cut down in the very city where prelates and barons were parleying over matters of peace and sovereignty, killed in trying to keep one faction from the throat of the other. At the very feet, as it were, of the bishop-legate. As black a sacrilege as if he had been butchered on the steps of the altar. It was not one man's death, it was a bitter symbol of the abandonment of law and the rejection of hope and reconciliation. So Radulfus had seen it, and so he recorded it in the offices of his house. There was a solemn acknowledgement due to the dead man, a memorial lodged in heaven.

'We are asked,' said Prior Robert, 'to offer thanks for the just endeavour and prayers for the soul of one Rainald Bossard, a knight in the service of the Empress Maud.'

*   *   *

'One of the enemy,' said a young novice doubtfully, talking it over in the cloisters afterwards. So used were they, in this shire, to thinking of the king's cause as their own, since

21

it had been his writ which had run here now in orderly fashion for four years, and kept off the worst of the chaos that troubled so much of England elsewhere.

'Not so,' said Brother Paul, the master of the novices, gently chiding. 'No good and honourable man is an enemy, though he may take the opposing side in this dissension. The fealty of this world is not for us, but we must bear it ever in mind as a true value, as binding on those who owe it as our vows are on us. The claims of these two cousins are both in some sort valid. It is no reproach to have kept faith, whether with king or empress. And this was surely a worthy man, or Father Abbot would not thus have recommended him to our prayers.'

Brother Anselm, thoughtfully revolving the syllables of the name, and tapping the resultant rhythm on the stone of the bench on which he sat, repeated to himself softly: 'Rainald Bossard, Rainald Bossard . . .'

The repeated iambic stayed in Brother Cadfael's ear and wormed its way into his mind. A name that meant nothing yet to anyone here, had neither form nor face, no age, no character; nothing but a name, which is either a soul without a body or a body without a soul. It went with him into his cell in the dortoir, as he made his last prayers and shook off his sandals before lying down to sleep. It may even have kept a rhythm in his sleeping mind, without the need of a dream to house it, for the first he knew of the thunder-storm was a silent double-gleam of lightning that spelled out the same iambic, and caused him to start awake with eyes still closed, and listen for the answering thunder. It did not come for so long that he thought he had dreamed it, and then he heard it, very distant, very quiet, and yet curiously ominous. Beyond his closed eyelids the quiet lightnings flared and died, and the echoes answered so late and so softly, from so far away . . .

As far, perhaps, as that fabled city of Winchester, where momentous matters had been decided, a place Cadfael had never seen, and probably never would see. A threat from a town so distant could shake no foundations here, and no hearts, any more than such far-off thunders could bring down the walls of Shrewsbury. Yet the continuing murmur of disquiet was still in his ears as he fell asleep.

CHAPTER TWO

Abbot Radulfus rode back into his abbey of Saint Peter and Saint Paul on the third day of June, escorted by his chaplain and secretary, Brother Vitalis, and welcomed home by all the fifty-three brothers, seven novices and six schoolboys of his house, as well as all the lay

23

stewards and servants.

The abbot was a long, lean, hard man in his fifties, with a gaunt, ascetic face and a shrewd, scholar's eye, so vigorous and able of body that he dismounted and went straight to preside at High Mass, before retiring to remove the stains of travel or take any refreshment after his long ride. Nor did he forget to offer the prayer he had enjoined upon his flock, for the repose of the soul of Rainald Bossard, slain in Winchester on the evening of Wednesday, the ninth day of April of this year of Our Lord 1141. Eight weeks dead, and half the length of England away, what meaning could Rainald Bossard have for this indifferent town of Shrewsbury, or the members of this far-distant Benedictine house?

Not until the next morning's chapter would the household hear its abbot's account of that momentous council held in the south to determine the future of England; but when Hugh Beringar waited upon Radulfus about mid-afternoon, and asked for audience, he was not kept waiting. Affairs demanded the close co-operation of the secular and the clerical powers, in defence of such order and law as survived in England.

The abbot's private parlour in his lodging was as austere as its presiding father, plainly furnished, but with sunlight spilled across its flagged floor from two open lattices at this hour of the sun's zenith, and a view of gracious

24

greenery and glowing flowers in the small walled garden without. Quiverings of radiance flashed and vanished and recoiled and collided over the dark panelling within, from the new-budded life and fresh breeze and exuberant light outside. Hugh sat in shadow, and watched the abbot's trenchant profile, clear, craggy and dark against a ground of shifting brightness.

'My allegiance is well known to you, Father,' said Hugh, admiring the stillness of the noble mask thus framed, 'as yours is to me. But there is much that we share. Whatever you can tell me of what passed in Winchester, I do greatly need to know.'

'And I to understand,' said Radulfus, with a tight and rueful smile. 'I went as summoned, by him who has a right to summon me, and I went knowing how matters then stood, the king a prisoner, the empress mistress of much of the south, and in due position to claim sovereignty by right of conquest. We knew, you and I both, what would be in debate down there. I can only give you my own account as I saw it. The first day that we gathered there, a Monday it was, the seventh of April, there was nothing done by way of business but the ceremonial of welcoming us all, and reading out—there were many of these!—the letters sent by way of excuse from those who remained absent. The empress had a lodging in the town then, though she made several moves about the region, to Reading and other

25

places, while we debated. She did not attend. She has a measure of discretion.' His tone was dry. It was not clear whether he considered her measure of that commodity to be adequate or somewhat lacking. 'The second day . . .' He fell silent, remembering what he had witnessed. Hugh waited attentively, not stirring.

'The second day, the eighth of April, the legate made his great speech . . .'

It was no effort to imagine him. Henry of Blois, bishop of Winchester, papal legate, younger brother and hitherto partisan of King Stephen, impregnably ensconced in the chapter house of his own cathedral, secure master of the political pulse of England, the cleverest manipulator in the kingdom, and on his own chosen ground—and yet hounded on to the defensive, in so far as that could ever happen to so expert a practitioner. Hugh had never seen the man, never been near the region where he ruled, had only heard him described, and yet could see him now, presiding with imperious composure over his half-unwilling assembly. A difficult part he had to play, to extricate himself from his known allegiance to his brother, and yet preserve his face and his status and influence with those who had shared it. And with a tough, experienced woman narrowly observing his every word, and holding in reserve her own new powers to destroy or preserve, according to how he managed his ill-disciplined team in this heavy furrow.

'He spoke a tedious while,' said the abbot candidly, 'but he is a very able speaker. He put us in mind that we were met together to try to salvage England from chaos and ruin. He spoke of the late King Henry's time, when order and peace was kept throughout the land. And he reminded us how the old king, left without a son, commanded his barons to swear an oath of allegiance to his only remaining child, his daughter Maud the empress, now widowed, and wed again to the count of Anjou.'

And so those barons had done, almost all, not least this same Henry of Winchester. Hugh Beringar, who had never come to such a test until he was ready to choose for himself, curled a half-disdainful and half-commiserating lip, and nodded understanding. 'His lordship had somewhat to explain away.'

The abbot refrained from indicating, by word or look, agreement with the implied criticism of his brother cleric. 'He said that the long delay which might then have arisen from the empress's being in Normandy had given rise to natural concern for the well-being of the state. An interim of uncertainty was dangerous. And thus, he said, his brother Count Stephen was accepted when he offered himself, and became king by consent. His own part in this acceptance he admitted. For he it was who pledged his word to God and men

27

that King Stephen would honour and revere the Holy Church, and maintain the good and just laws of the land. In which undertaking, said Henry, the king has shamefully failed. To his great chagrin and grief he declared it, having been his brother's guarantor to God.'

So that was the way round the humiliating change of course, thought Hugh. All was to be laid upon Stephen, who had so deceived his reverend brother and defaulted upon all his promises, that a man of God might well be driven to the end of his patience, and be brought to welcome a change of monarch with relief tempering his sorrow.

'In particular,' said Radulfus, 'he recalled how the king had hounded certain of his bishops to their ruin and death.'

There was more than a grain of truth in that, though the only death in question, of Robert of Salisbury, had resulted naturally from old age, bitterness and despair, because his power was gone.

'Therefore, *he said*,' continued the abbot with chill deliberation, 'the judgement of God had been manifested against the king, in delivering him up prisoner to his enemies. And he, devout in the service of the Holy Church, must choose between his devotion to his mortal brother and to his immortal father, and could not but bow to the edict of heaven. Therefore he had called us together, to ensure that a kingdom lopped of its head should not

28

founder in utter ruin. And this very matter, he told the assembly, had been discussed most gravely on the day previous among the greater part of the clergy of England, who—*he said!*—had a prerogative surmounting others in the election and consecration of a king.'

There was something in the dry, measured voice that made Hugh prick up his ears. For this was a large and unprecedented claim, and by all the signs Abbot Radulfus found it more than suspect. The legate had his own face to save, and a well-oiled tongue with which to wind the protective mesh of words before it.

'Was there such a meeting? Were you present at such, Father?'

'There was a meeting,' said Radulfus, 'not prolonged, and by no means very clear in its course. The greater part of the talking was done by the legate. The empress had her partisans there.' He said it sedately and tolerantly, but clearly he had not been one. 'I do not recall that he then claimed this prerogative for us. Nor that there was ever a count taken.'

'Nor, as I guess, declared. It would not come to a numbering of heads or hands.' Too easy, then, to start a counter-count of one's own, and confound the reckoning.

'He continued,' said Radulfus coolly and drily, 'by saying that we had chosen as Lady of England the late king's daughter, the inheritor of his nobility and his will to peace. As the sire was unequalled in merit in our times, so might his daughter flourish and bring peace, as he did, to this troubled country, where we now offer her—*he said!*—our whole-hearted fealty.'

So the legate had extricated himself as adroitly as possible from his predicament. But for all that, so resolute, courageous and vindictive a lady as the empress was going to look somewhat sidewise at a whole-hearted fealty which had already once been pledged to her, and turned its back nimbly under pressure, and might as nimbly do so again. If she was wise she would curb her resentment and take care to keep on the right side of the legate, as he was cautiously feeling his way to the right side of her; but she would not forget or forgive.

'And there was no man raised a word against it?' asked Hugh mildly.

'None. There was small opportunity, and even less inducement. And with that the bishop announced that he had invited a deputation from the city of London, and expected them to arrive that day, so that it was expedient we should adjourn our discussion until the morrow. Even so, the Londoners did not come until next day, and we met again somewhat later than on the days previous. Howbeit, they did come. With somewhat dour faces and stiff necks. They said that they represented the whole commune of London, into which many barons had also entered as

30

members after Lincoln, and that they all, with no wish to challenge the legitimacy of our assembly, yet desired to put forward with one voice the request that the lord king should be set at liberty.'

'That was bold,' said Hugh with raised brows. 'How did his lordship counter it? Was he put out of countenance?'

'I think he was shaken, but not disastrously, not then. He made a long speech—it is a way of keeping others silent, at least for a time— reproving the city for taking into its membership men who had abandoned their king in war, after leading him astray by their evil advice, so grossly that he forsook God and right, and was brought to the judgement of defeat and captivity, from which the prayers of those same false friends could not now reprieve him. These men do but flatter and favour you now, he said, for their own advantage.'

'If he meant the Flemings who ran from Lincoln,' Hugh allowed, 'he told no more than truth there. But for what other end is the city ever flattered and wooed? What then? Had they the hardihood to stand their ground against him?'

'They were in some disarray as to what they should reply, and went apart to confer. And while there was quiet, a man suddenly stepped forward from among the clerks, and held out a parchment to Bishop Henry, asking him to read it aloud, so confidently that I wonder still he did not at once comply. Instead, he opened and began to read it in silence, and in a moment more he was thundering in a great rage that the thing was an insult to the reverend company present, its matter disgraceful, its witnesses attainted enemies of Holy Church, and not a word of it would he read aloud to us in so sacred a place as his chapter house. Whereupon,' said the abbot grimly, 'the clerk snatched it back from him, and himself read it aloud in a great voice, riding above the bishop when he tried to silence him. It was a plea from Stephen's queen to all present, and to the legate in especial, own brother to the king, to return to fealty and restore the king to his own again from the base captivity into which traitors had betrayed him. And I, said the brave man who read, am a clerk in the service of Queen Matilda, and if any ask my name, it is Christian, and true Christian I am as any here, and true to my salt.'

'Brave, indeed!' said Hugh, and whistled softly. 'But I doubt it did him little good.'

'The legate replied to him in a tirade, much as he had spoken already to us the day before, but in a great passion, and so intimidated the men from London that they drew in their horns, and grudgingly agreed to report the council's election to their citizens, and support it as best they could. As for the man Christian, who had so angered Bishop Henry, he was attacked that same evening in the street, as he set out to return to the queen empty-handed. Four or five ruffians set on him in the dark, no one knows who, for they fled when one of the empress's knights and his men came to the rescue and beat them off, crying shame to use murder as argument in any cause, and against an honest man who had done his part fearlessly in the open. The clerk got no worse than a few bruises. It was the knight who got the knife between his ribs from behind and into the heart. He died in the gutter of a Winchester street. A shame to us all, who claim to be making peace and bringing enemies into amity.'

By the shadowed anger of his face it had gone deep with him, the single wanton act that denied all pretences of good will and justice and conciliation. To strike at a man for being honestly of the opposite persuasion, and then to strike again at the fair-minded and chivalrous who sought to prevent the outrage—very ill omens, these, for the future of the legate's peace.

'And no man taken for the killing?' demanded Hugh, frowning.

'No. They fled in the dark. If any creature knows name or hiding-place, he has spoken no word. Death is so common a matter now, even by stealth and treachery in the darkness, this will be forgotten with the rest. And the next day our council closed with sentence of excommunication against a great number of Stephen's men, and the legate pronounced all men blessed who would bless the empress, and accursed those who cursed her. And so dismissed us,' said Radulfus. 'But that we monastics were not dismissed, but kept to attend on him some weeks longer.'

'And the empress?'

'Withdrew to Oxford, while these long negotiations with the city of London went on, how and when she should be admitted within the gates, on what terms, what numbers she might bring in with her to Westminster. On all which points they have wrangled every step of the way. But in nine or ten days now she will be installed there, and soon thereafter crowned.' He lifted a long, muscular hand, and again let it fall into the lap of his habit. 'So, at least, it seems. What more can I tell you of her?'

'I meant, rather,' said Hugh, 'how is she bearing this slow recognition? How is she dealing with her newly converted barons? And how do they rub, one with another? It's no easy matter to hold together the old and the new liegemen, and keep them from each other's throats. A manor in dispute here and there, a few fields taken from one and given to another ... I think you know the way of it, Father, as well as I.'

'I would not say she is a wise woman,' said

Radulfus carefully. 'She is all too well aware how many swore allegiance to her at her father's order, and then swung to King Stephen, and now as nimbly skip back to her because she is in the ascendant. I can well understand she might take pleasure in pricking into the quick where she can, among these. It is not wise, but it is human. But that she should become lofty and cold to those who never wavered—for there are some,' said the abbot with respectful wonder, 'who have been faithful throughout at their own great loss, and will not waver even now, whatever she may do. Great folly and great injustice to use them so high-handedly, who have been her right hand and her left all this while.'

You comfort me, thought Hugh, watching the lean, quiet face intently. The woman is out of her wits if she flouts even the like of Robert of Gloucester, now she feels herself so near the throne.

'She has greatly offended the bishop-legate,' said the abbot, 'by refusing to allow Stephen's son to receive the rights and titles of his father's honours of Boulogne and Mortain, now that his father is a prisoner. It would have been only justice. But no, she would not suffer it. Bishop Henry quit her court for some while, it took her considerable pains to lure him back again.'

Better and better, thought Hugh, assessing his position with care. If she is stubborn

35

enough to drive away even Henry, she can undo everything he and others do for her. Put the crown in her hands and she may, not so much drop it, as hurl it at someone against whom she has a score to settle. He set himself to extract every detail of her subsequent behaviour, and was cautiously encouraged. She had taken land from some who held it and given it to others. She had received her naturally bashful new adherents with arrogance, and reminded them ominously of their past hostility. Some she had even repulsed with anger, recalling old injuries. Candidates for a disputed crown should be more accommodatingly forgetful. Let her alone, and pray! She, if anyone, could bring about her own ruin.

At the end of a long hour he rose to take his leave, with a very fair picture in his mind of the possibilities he had to face. Even empresses may learn, and she might yet inveigle herself safely into Westminster and assume the crown. It would not do to underestimate William of Normandy's grand-daughter and Henry the First's daughter. Yet that very stock might come to wreck on its own unforgiving strength.

He was never afterwards sure why he turned back at the last moment to ask: 'Father Abbot, this man Rainald Bossard, who died ... A knight of the empress, you said. In whose following?'

*   *   *

All that he had learned he confided to Brother
Cadfael in the hut in the herb-garden, trying
out upon his friend's unexcitable solidity his
own impressions and doubts, like a man
sharpening a scythe on a good memorial stone.
Cadfael was fussing over a too-exuberant wine,
and seemed not to be listening, but Hugh
remained undeceived. His friend had a sharp
ear cocked for every intonation, even turned a
swift glance occasionally to confirm what his
ear heard, and reckon up the double account.

'You'd best lean back, then,' said Cadfael
finally, 'and watch what will follow. You might
also, I suppose, have a good man take a look at
Bristol? He is the only hostage she has. With
the king loosed, or Robert, or Brian
FitzCount, or some other of sufficient note
made prisoner to match him, you'd be on
secure ground. God forgive me, why am I
advising you, who have no prince in this
world!' But he was none too sure about the
truth of that, having had brief, remembered
dealings with Stephen himself, and liked the
man, even at his ill-advised worst, when he had
slaughtered the garrison of Shrewsbury castle,
to regret it as long as his ebullient memory
kept nudging him with the outrage. By now, in
his dungeon in Bristol, he might well have
forgotten the uncharacteristic savagery.

'And do you know,' asked Hugh with

37

deliberation, 'whose man was this knight Rainald Bossard, left bleeding to death in the lanes of Winchester? He for whom your prayers have been demanded?'

Cadfael turned from his boisterously bubbling jar to narrow his eyes on his friend's face. 'The empress's man is all we've been told. But I see you're about to tell me more.'

'He was in the following of Laurence d'Angers.'

Cadfael straightened up with incautious haste, and grunted at the jolt to his ageing back. It was the name of a man neither of them had ever set eyes on, yet it started vivid memories for them both.

'Yes, *that* Laurence! A baron of Gloucestershire, and liegeman to the empress. One of the few who has not once turned his coat yet in this to-ing and fro-ing, and uncle to those two children you helped away from Bromfield to join him, when they went astray after the sack of Worcester. Do you still remember the cold of that winter? And the wind that scoured away hills of snow overnight and laid them down in fresh places before morning? I still feel it, clean through flesh and bone . . .'

There was nothing about that winter journey that Cadfael would ever forget. [See *The Virgin in the Ice*.] It was hardly a year and a half past, the attack on the city of Worcester, the flight of brother and sister northwards

38

towards Shrewsbury, through the worst weather for many a year. Laurence d'Angers had been but a name in the business, as he was now in this. An adherent of the Empress Maud, he had been denied leave to enter King Stephen's territory to search for his young kin, but he had sent a squire in secret to find and fetch them away. To have borne a hand in the escape of those three was something to remember lifelong. All three arose living before Cadfael's mind's eye, the boy Yves, thirteen years old then, ingenuous and gallant and endearing, jutting a stubborn Norman chin at danger, his elder sister Ermina, newly shaken into womanhood and resolutely shouldering the consequences of her own follies. And the third . . .

'I have often wondered,' said Hugh thoughtfully, 'how they fared afterwards. I knew you would get them off safely, if I left it to you, but it was still a perilous road before them. I wonder if we shall ever get word. Some day the world will surely hear of Yves Hugonin.' At the thought of the boy he smiled with affectionate amusement. 'And that dark lad who fetched them away, he who dressed like a woodsman and fought like a paladin . . . I fancy you knew more of him than ever I got to know.'

Cadfael smiled into the glow of the brazier and did not deny it. 'So his lord is there in the empress's train, is he? And this knight who was killed was in d'Angers' service? That was a very ill thing, Hugh.'

'So Abbot Radulfus thinks,' said Hugh sombrely.

'In the dusk and in confusion—and all got clean away, even the one who used the knife. A foul thing, for surely that was no chance blow. The clerk Christian escaped out of their hands, yet one among them turned on the rescuer before he fled. It argues a deal of hate at being thwarted, to have ventured that last moment before running. And is it left so? And Winchester full of those who should most firmly stand for justice?'

'Why, some among them would surely have been well enough pleased if that bold clerk had spilled his blood in the gutter, as well as the knight. Some may well have set the hunt on him.'

'Well for the empress's good name,' said Cadfael, 'that there was one at least of her men stout enough to respect an honest opponent, and stand by him to the death. And shame if that death goes unpaid for.'

'Old friend,' said Hugh ruefully, rising to take his leave, 'England has had to swallow many such a shame these last years. It grows customary to sigh and shrug and forget. At which, as I know, you are a very poor hand. And I have seen you overturn custom more than once, and been glad of it. But not even you can do much now for Rainald Bossard, bar praying for his soul. It is a very long way from here to Winchester.'

'It is not so far,' said Cadfael, as much to himself as to his friend, 'not by many a mile, as it was an hour since.'

*   *   *

He went to Vespers, and to supper in the refectory, and thereafter to Collations and Compline, and all with one remembered face before his mind's eye, so that he paid but fractured attention to the readings, and had difficulty in concentrating his thoughts on prayer. Though it might have been a kind of prayer he was offering throughout, in gratitude and praise and humility.

So suave, so young, so dark and vital a face, startling in its beauty when he had first seen it over the girl's shoulder, the face of the young squire sent to bring away the Hugonin children to their uncle and guardian. A long, spare, wide-browed face, with a fine scimitar of a nose and a supple bow of a mouth, and the fierce, fearless, golden eyes of a hawk. A head capped closely with curving, blue-black hair, coiling crisply at his temples and clasping his cheeks like folded wings. So young and yet so formed a face, east and west at home in it, shaven clean like a Norman, olive-skinned like a Syrian, all his memories of the Holy Land in one human countenance. The favourite squire of Laurence d'Angers, come home with him from the Crusade. Olivier de Bretagne.

If his lord was there in the south with his following, in the empress's retinue, where else would Olivier be? The abbot might even have rubbed shoulders with him, unbeknown, or seen him ride past at his lord's elbow, and for one absent moment admired his beauty. Few such faces blaze out of the humble mass of our ordinariness, thought Cadfael, the finger of God cannot choose but mark them out for notice, and his officers here will be the first to recognise and own them.

And this Rainald Bossard who is dead, an honourable man doing right by an honourable opponent, was Olivier's comrade, owning the same lord and pledged to the same service. His death will be grief to Olivier. Grief to Olivier is grief to me, a wrong done to Olivier is a wrong done to me. As far away as Winchester may be, here am I left mourning in that dark street where a man died for a generous act, in which, by the same token, he did not fail, for the clerk Christian lived on to return to his lady, the queen, with his errand faithfully done.

The gentle rustlings and stirrings of the dortoir sighed into silence outside the frail partitions of Cadfael's cell long before he rose from his knees, and shook off his sandals. The little lamp by the night stairs cast only the faintest gleam across the beams of the roof, a ceiling of pearly grey above the darkness of his

42

cell, his home now for—was it eighteen years or nineteen?—he had difficulty in recalling. It was as if a part of him, heart, mind, soul, whatever that essence might be, had not so much retired as come home to take seisin of a heritage here, his from his birth. And yet he remembered and acknowledged with gratitude and joy the years of his sojourning in the world, the lusty childhood and venturous youth, the taking of the Cross and the passion of the Crusade, the women he had known and loved, the years of his sea-faring off the coast of the Holy Kingdom of Jerusalem, all that pilgrimage that had led him here at last to his chosen retreat. None of it wasted, however foolish and amiss, nothing lost, nothing vain, all of it somehow fitting him to the narrow niche where now he served and rested. God had given him a sign, he had no need to regret anything, only to lay all open and own it his. For God's viewing, not for man's.

He lay quiet in the darkness, straight and still like a man coffined, but easy, with his arms lax at his sides, and his half-closed eyes dreaming on the vault above him, where the faint light played among the beams.

There was no lightning that night, only a consort of steady rolls of thunder both before and after Matins and Lauds, so unalarming that many among the brothers failed to notice them. Cadfael heard them as he rose, and as he returned to his rest. They seemed to him a

43

reminder and a reassurance that Winchester had indeed moved nearer to Shrewsbury, and consoled him that his grievance was not overlooked, but noted in heaven, and he might look to have his part yet in collecting the debt due to Rainald Bossard. Upon which warranty, he fell asleep.

CHAPTER THREE

On the seventeenth day of June Saint Winifred's elaborate oak coffin, silver-ornamented and lined with lead behind all its immaculate seals, was removed from its place of honour and carried with grave and subdued ceremony back to its temporary resting-place in the chapel of the hospital of Saint Giles, there to wait, as once before, for the auspicious day, the twenty-second of June. The weather was fair, sunny and still, barely a cloud in the sky, and yet cool enough for travelling, the best of weather for pilgrims. And by the eighteenth day the pilgrims began to arrive, a scattering of fore-runners before the full tide began to flow.

Brother Cadfael had watched the reliquary depart on its memorial journey with a slightly guilty mind, for all his honest declaration that he could hardly have done otherwise than he had done, there in the summer night in

Gwytherin. So strongly had he felt, above all, her Welshness, the feeling she must have for the familiar tongue about her, and the tranquil flow of the seasons in her solitude, where she had slept so long and so well in her beatitude, and worked so many small, sweet miracles for her own people. No, he could not believe he had made a wrong choice there. If only she would glance his way, and smile, and say, well done!

The very first of the pilgrims came probing into the walled herb-garden, with Brother Denis's directions to guide him, in search of a colleague in his own mystery. Cadfael was busy weeding the close-planted beds of mint and thyme and sage late in the afternoon, a tedious, meticulous labour in the ripeness of a favourable June, after spring sun and shower had been nicely balanced, and growth was a green battlefield. He backed out of a cleansed bed, and backed into a solid form, rising startled from his knees to turn and face a rusty black brother shaped very much like himself, though probably fifteen years younger. They stood at gaze, two solid, squarely built brethren of the Order, eyeing each other in instant recognition and acknowledgement.

'You must be Brother Cadfael,' said the stranger-brother in a broad, melodious bass voice. 'Brother Hospitaller told me where to find you. My name is Adam, a brother of Reading. I have the very charge there that you bear here, and I have heard tell of you, even as far south as my house.'

His eye was roving, as he spoke, towards some of Cadfael's rarer treasures, the eastern poppies he had brought from the Holy Land and reared here with anxious care, the delicate fig that still contrived to thrive against the sheltering north wall, where the sun nursed it. Cadfael warmed to him for the quickening of his eye, and the mild greed that flushed the round, shaven face. A sturdy, stalwart man, who moved as if confident of his body, one who might prove a man of his hands if challenged. Well-weathered, too, a genuine outdoor man.

'You're more than welcome, brother,' said Cadfael heartily. 'You'll be here for the saint's feast? And have they found you a place in the dortoir? There are a few cells vacant, for any of our own who come, like you.'

'My abbot sent me from Reading with a mission to our daughter house of Leominster,' said Brother Adam, probing with an experimental toe into the rich, well-fed loam of Brother Cadfael's bed of mint, and raising an eyebrow respectfully at the quality he found. 'I asked if I might prolong the errand to attend on the translation of Saint Winifred, and I was given the needful permission. It's seldom I could hope to be sent so far north, and it would be pity to miss such an opportunity.'

46

'And they've found you a brother's bed?' Such a man, Benedictine, gardener and herbalist, could not be wasted on a bed in the guest-hall. Cadfael coveted him, marking the bright eye with which the newcomer singled out his best endeavours.

'Brother Hospitaller was so gracious. I am placed in a cell close to the novices.'

'We shall be near neighbours,' said Cadfael contentedly. 'Now come, I'll show you whatever we have here to show, for the main garden is on the far side of the Foregate, along the bank of the river. But here I keep my own herber. And if there should be anything here that can be safely carried to Reading, you may take cuttings most gladly before you leave us.'

They fell into a very pleasant and voluble discussion, perambulating all the walks of the closed garden, and comparing experiences in cultivation and use. Brother Adam of Reading had a sharp eye for rarities, and was likely to go home laden with spoils. He admired the neatness and order of Cadfael's workshop, the collection of rustling bunches of dried herbs hung from the roof-beams and under the eaves, and the array of bottles, jars and flagons along the shelves. He had hints and tips of his own to propound, too, and the amiable contest kept them happy all the afternoon. When they returned together to the great court before Vespers it was to a scene notably animated, as if the bustle of celebration was already

47

beginning. There were horses being led down into the stableyard, and bundles being carried in at the guest-hall. A stout elderly man, well equipped for riding, paced across towards the church to pay his first respects on arrival, with a servant trotting at his heels.

Brother Paul's youngest charges, all eyes and curiosity, ringed the gatehouse to watch the early arrivals, and were shooed aside by Brother Jerome, very busy as usual with all the prior's errands. Though the boys did not go very far, and formed their ring again as soon as Jerome was out of sight. A few of the citizens of the Foregate had gathered in the street to watch, excited dogs running among their legs.

'Tomorrow,' said Cadfael, eyeing the scene, 'there will be many more. This is but the beginning. Now if the weather stays fair we shall have a very fine festival for our saint.'

And she will understand that all is in her honour, he thought privately, even if she does lie very far from here. And who knows whether she may not pay us a visit, out of the kindness of her heart? What is distance to a saint, who can be where she wills in the twinkling of an eye?

*   *   *

The guest-hall filled steadily on the morrow. All day long they came, some singly, some in groups as they had met and made comfortable

48

acquaintance on the road, some afoot, some on ponies, some whole and hearty and on holiday, some who had travelled only a few miles, some who came from far away, and among them a number who went on crutches, or were led along by better-sighted friends, or had grievous deformities or skin diseases, or debilitating illnesses; and all these hoping for relief.

Cadfael went about the regular duties of his day, divided between church and herbarium, but with an interested eye open for all there was to see whenever he crossed the great court, boiling now with activity. Every arriving figure, every face, engaged his notice, but as yet distantly, none being provided with a name, to make him individual. Such of them as needed his services for relief would be directed to him, such as came his way by chance would be entitled to his whole attention, freely offered.

It was the woman he noticed first, bustling across the court from the gatehouse to the guest-hall with a basket on her arm, fresh from the Foregate market with new-baked bread and little cakes, soon after Prime. A careful housewife, to be off marketing so early even on holiday, decided about what she wanted, and not content to rely on the abbey bakehouse to provide it. A sturdy, confident figure of a woman, perhaps fifty years of age but in full rosy bloom. Her dress was sober and

49

plain, but of good material and proudly kept, her wimple snow-white beneath her head-cloth of brown linen. She was not tall, but so erect that she could pass for tall, and her face was round, wide-eyed and broad-cheeked, with a determined chin to it.

She vanished briskly into the guest-hall, and he caught but a glimpse of her, but she was positive enough to stay with him through the offices and duties of the morning, and as the worshippers left the church after Mass he caught sight of her again, arms spread like a hen-wife driving her birds, marshalling two chicks, it seemed, before her, both largely concealed beyond her ample width and bountiful skirts. Indeed she had a general largeness about her, her head-dress surely taller and broader than need, her hips bolstered by petticoats, the aura of bustle and command she bore about with her equally generous and ebullient. He felt a wave of warmth go out to her for her energy and vigour, while he spared a morsel of sympathy for the chicks she mothered, stowed thus away beneath such ample, smothering wings.

In the afternoon, busy about his small kingdom and putting together the medicaments he must take along the Foregate to Saint Giles in the morning, to be sure they had provision enough over the feast, he was not thinking of her, nor of any of the inhabitants of the guest-hall, since none had as yet had occasion to call for his aid. He was packing lozenges into a small box, soothing tablets for scoured, dry throats, when a bulky shadow blocked the open door of his workshop, and a brisk, light voice said, 'Pray your pardon, brother, but Brother Denis advised me to come to you, and sent me here.'

And there she stood, filling the doorway, shoulders squared, hands folded at her waist, head braced and face full forward. Her eyes, wide and wide-set, were bright blue but meagrely supplied with pale lashes, yet very firm and fixed in their regard.

'It's my young nephew, you see, brother,' she went on confidently, 'my sister's son, that was fool enough to go off and marry a roving Welshman from Builth, and now her man's gone, and so is she, poor lass, and left her two children orphan, and nobody to care for them but me. And me with my own husband dead, and all his craft fallen to me to manage, and never a chick of my own to be my comfort. Not but what I can do very well with the work and the journeymen, for I've learned these twenty years what was what in the weaving trade, but still I could have done with a son of my own. But it was not to be, and a sister's son is dearly welcome, so he is, whether he has his health or no, for he's the dearest lad ever you saw. And it's the pain, you see, brother. I don't like to see him in pain, though he doesn't complain. So I'm come to you.'

Cadfael made haste to wedge a toe into this first chink in her volubility, and insert a few words of his own into the gap.

'Come within, mistress, and welcome. Tell me what's the nature of your lad's pain, and what I can do for you and him I'll do. But best I should see him and speak with him, for he best knows where he hurts. Sit down and be easy, and tell me about him.'

She came in confidently enough, and settled herself with a determined spreading of ample skirts on the bench against the wall. Her gaze went round the laden shelves, the stored herbs dangling, the brazier and the pots and flasks, interested and curious, but in no way awed by Cadfael or his mysteries.

'I'm from the cloth country down by Campden, brother, Weaver by name and by trade was my man, and his father and grandfather before him, and Alice Weaver is my name, and I keep up the work just as he did. But this young sister of mine, she went off with a Welshman, and the pair of them are dead now, and the children I sent for to live with me. The girl is eighteen years old now, a good, hard-working maid, and I daresay we shall contrive to find a decent match for her in the end, though I shall miss her help, for she's grown very handy, and is strong and healthy, not like the lad. Named for some outlandish Welsh saint, she is, Melangell, if ever you heard the like!'

'I'm Welsh myself,' said Cadfael cheerfully. 'Our Welsh names do come hard on your English tongues, I know.'

'Ah well, the boy brought a name with him that's short and simple enough. Rhun, they named him. Sixteen he is now, two years younger than his sister, but wants her heartiness, poor soul. He's well-grown enough, and very comely, but from a child something went wrong with his right leg, it's twisted and feebled so he can put but the very toe of it to the ground at all, and even that turned on one side, and can lay no weight on it, but barely touch. He goes on two crutches. And I've brought him here in the hope good Saint Winifred will do something for him. But it's cost him dear to make the walk, even though we started out three weeks ago, and have taken it by easy shifts.'

'He's walked the whole way?' asked Cadfael, dismayed.

'I'm not so prosperous I can afford a horse, more than the one they need for the business at home. Twice on the way a kind carter did give him a ride as far as he was bound, but the rest he's hobbled on his crutches. Many another at this feast, brother, will have done as much, in as bad case or worse. But he's here now, safe in the guest-hall, and if my prayers can do anything for him, he'll walk home again on two sound legs as ever held up a hale and hearty man. But now for these few days he

53

suffers as bad as before.'

'You should have brought him here with you,' said Cadfael. 'What's the nature of his pain? Is it in moving or when he lies still? Is it the bones of the leg that ache?'

'It's worst in his bed at night. At home I've often heard him weeping for pain in the night, though he tries to keep it so silent we need not be disturbed. Often he gets little or no sleep. His bones do ache, that's truth, but also the sinews of his calf knot into such cramps it makes him groan.'

'There can be something done about that,' said Cadfael, considering. 'At least we may try. And there are draughts can dull the pain and help him to a night's sleep, at any rate.'

'It isn't that I don't trust to the saint,' explained Mistress Weaver anxiously. 'But while he waits for her, let him be at rest if he can, that's what I say. Why should not a suffering lad seek help from ordinary decent mortals, too, good men like you who have faith and knowledge both?'

'Why not, indeed!' agreed Cadfael. 'The least of us may be an instrument of grace, though not by his own deserving. Better let the boy come to me here, where we can be private together. The guest-hall will be busy and noisy, here we shall have quiet.'

She rose, satisfied, to take her leave, but she had plenty yet to say even in departing of the long, slow journey, the small kindnesses they

54

had met with on the way, and the fellow pilgrims, some of whom had passed them and arrived here before them.

'There's more than one in there,' said she, wagging her head towards the lofty rear wall of the guest-hall, 'will be needing your help, besides my Rhun. There were two young fellows we came along with the last days, we could keep pace with them, for they were slowed much as we were. Oh, the one of them was hale and lusty enough, but would not stir a step ahead of his friend, and that poor soul had come barefoot more miles even than Rhun had come crippled, and his feet a sight for pity, but would he so much as bind them with rags? Not he! He said he was under vow to go unshod to his journey's end. And a great heavy cross on a string round his neck, too, and he rubbed raw with the chafing of it, but that was part of his vow, too. I see no reason why a fine young fellow should choose such a torment of his own will, but there, folk do strange things, I daresay he hopes to win some great mercy for himself with his austerities. Still, I should think he might at least get some balm for his feet, while he's here at rest? Shall I bid him come to you? I'd gladly do a small service for that pair. The other one, Matthew, the sturdy one, he hefted my girl safe out of the way of harm when some mad horsemen in a hurry all but rode us down into the ditch, and he carried our bundles for her after, for she was well loaded, I being busy helping Rhun along. Truth to tell, I think the young man was taken with our Melangell, for he was very attentive to her once we joined company. More than to his friend, though indeed he never stirred a step away from him. A vow is a vow, I suppose, and if a man's taken all that suffering on himself of his own will, what can another do to prevent it? No more than bear him company, and that the lad is doing, faithfully, for he never leaves him.'

She was out of the door and spreading appreciative nostrils for the scent of the sunlit herbs, when she looked back to add: 'There's others among them may call themselves pilgrims as loud and often as they will, but I wouldn't trust one or two of them as far as I could throw them. I suppose rogues will make their way everywhere, even among the saints.'

'As long as the saints have money in their purses, or anything about them worth stealing,' agreed Cadfael wryly, 'rogues will never be far away.'

Whether Mistress Weaver did speak to her strange travelling companion or not, it was he who arrived at Cadfael's workshop within half an hour, before ever the boy Rhun showed his face. Cadfael was back at his weeding when he heard them come, or heard, rather, the slow, patient footsteps of the sturdy one stirring the gravel of his pathways. The other made no sound in walking, for he stepped tenderly and carefully in the grass border, which was cool and kind to his misused feet. If there was any sound to betray his coming it was the long, effortful sighing of his breath, the faint, indrawn hiss of pain. As soon as Cadfael straightened his back and turned his head, he knew who came.

They were much of an age, and even somewhat alike in build and colouring, above middle height but that the one stooped in his laboured progress, brown-haired and dark of eye, and perhaps twenty-five or twenty-six years old. Yet not so like that they could have been brothers or close kin. The hale one had the darker complexion, as though he had been more in the air and the sun, and broader bones of cheek and jaw, a stubborn, proud, secret face, disconcertingly still, confiding nothing. The sufferer's face was long, mobile and passionate, with high cheekbones and hollow cheeks beneath them, and a mouth tight-drawn, either with present pain or constant passion. Anger might be one of his customary companions, burning ardour another. The young man Matthew stalked at his heels mute and jealously watchful in attendance on him.

Mindful of Mistress Weaver's loquacious confidences, Cadfael looked from the scarred and swollen feet to the chafed neck. Within the collar of his plain dark coat the votary had wound a length of linen cloth, to alleviate the rubbing of the thin cord from which a heavy

57

cross of iron, chaced in a leaf pattern with what looked like gold, hung down upon his breast. By the look of the seam of red that marked the linen, either this padding was new, or else it had not been effective. The cord was mercilessly thin, the cross certainly heavy. To what desperate end could a young man choose so to torture himself? And what pleasure did he think it could give to God or Saint Winifred to contemplate his discomfort?

Eyes feverishly bright scanned him. A low voice asked: 'You are Brother Cadfael? That is the name Brother Hospitaller gave me. He said you would have ointments and salves that could be of help to me. So far,' he added, eyeing Cadfael with glittering fixity, 'as there is any help anywhere for me.'

Cadfael gave him a considering look for that, but asked nothing until he had marshalled the pair of them into his workshop and sat the sufferer down to be inspected with due care. The young man Matthew took up his stand beside the open door, careful to avoid blocking the light, but would not come further within.

'You've come a fairish step unshod,' said Cadfael, on his knees to examine the damage. 'Was such cruelty needful?'

'It was. I do not hate myself so much as to bear this to no purpose.' The silent youth by the door stirred slightly, but said no word. 'I am under vow,' said his companion, 'and will

58

not break it.' It seemed that he felt a need to account for himself, forestalling questioning. 'My name is Ciaran, I am of a Welsh mother, and I am going back to where I was born, there to end my life as I began it. You see the wounds on my feet, brother, but what most ails me does not show anywhere upon me. I have a fell disease, no threat to any other, but it must shortly end me.'

And it could be true, thought Cadfael, busy with a cleansing oil on the swollen soles, and the toes cut by gravel and stones. The feverish fire of the deep-set eyes might well mean an even fiercer fire within. True, the young body, now eased in repose, was well-made and had not lost flesh, but that was no sure proof of health. Ciaran's voice remained low, level and firm. If he knew he had his death, he had come to terms with it.

'So I am returning in penitential pilgrimage, for my soul's health, which is of greater import. Barefoot and burdened I shall walk to the house of canons at Aberdaron, so that after my death I may be buried on the holy isle of Ynys Enlli, where the soil is made up of the bones and dust of thousands upon thousands of saints.'

'I should have thought,' said Cadfael mildly, 'that such a privilege could be earned by going there shod and tranquil and humble, like any other man.' But for all that, it was an understandable ambition for a devout man of

59

Welsh extraction, knowing his end near. Aberdaron, at the tip of the Lleyn peninsula, fronting the wild sea and the holiest island of the Welsh church, had been the last resting place of many, and the hospitality of the canons of the house was never refused to any man. 'I would not cast doubt on your sacrifice, but self-imposed suffering seems to me a kind of arrogance, and not humility.'

'It may be so,' said Ciaran remotely. 'No help for it now, I am bound.'

'That is true,' said Matthew from his corner by the door. A measured and yet an abrupt voice, deeper than his companion's. 'Fast bound! So are we both, I no less than he.'

'Hardly by the same vows,' said Cadfael drily. For Matthew wore good, solid shoes, a little down at heel, but proof against the stones of the road.

'No, not the same. But no less binding. And I do not forget mine, any more than he forgets his.'

Cadfael laid down the foot he had anointed, setting a folded cloth under it, and lifted its fellow into his lap. 'God forbid I should tempt any man to break his oath. You will both do as you must do. But at least you may rest your feet here until after the feast, which will give you three days for healing, and here within the pale the ground is not so harsh. And once healed, I have a rough spirit that will help to harden your soles for when you take to the road again. Why not, unless you have forsworn all help from men? And since you came to me, I take it you have not yet gone so far. There, sit a while longer, and let that dry.'

He rose from his knees, surveying his work critically, and turned his attention next to the linen wrapping about Ciaran's neck. He laid both hands gently on the cord by which the cross depended, and made to lift it over the young man's head.

'No, no, let be!' It was a soft, wild cry of alarm, and Ciaran clutched at cross and cord, one with either hand, and hugged his burden to him fiercely. 'Don't touch it! Let it be!'

'Surely,' said Cadfael, startled, 'you may lift it off while I dress the wound it's cost you? Hardly a moment's work, why not?'

'No!' Ciaran fastened both hands upon the cross and hugged it to his breast. 'No, never for a moment, night or day! No! Let it alone!'

'Lift it, then,' said Cadfael resignedly, 'and hold it while I dress this cut. No, never fear, I'll not cheat you. Only let me unwind this cloth, and see what damage you have there, hidden.'

'Yet he should doff it, and so I have prayed him constantly,' said Matthew softly. 'How else can he be truly rid of his pains?'

Cadfael unwound the linen, viewed the scored line of half-dried blood, still oozing, and went to work on it with a stinging lotion first to clean it of dust and fragments of frayed skin, and then with a healing ointment of

61

cleavers. He refolded the cloth, and wound it carefully under the cord. 'There, you have not broken faith. Settle your load again. If you hold up the weight in your hands as you go, and loosen it in your bed, you'll be rid of your gash before you depart.'

It seemed to him that they were both of them in haste to leave him, for the one set his feet tenderly to ground as soon as he was released, holding up the weight of his cross obediently with both hands, and the other stepped out through the doorway into the sunlit garden, and waited on guard for his friend to emerge. The one owed no special thanks, the other offered only the merest acknowledgement.

'But I would remind you both,' said Cadfael, and with a thoughtful eye on both, 'that you are now present at the feast of a saint who has worked many miracles, even to the defiance of death. One who may have life itself within her gift,' he said strongly, 'even for a man already condemned to death. Bear it in mind, for she may be listening now!'

They said never a word, neither did they look at each other. They stared back at him from the scented brightness of the garden with startled, wary eyes, and then they turned abruptly as one man, and limped and strode away.

CHAPTER FOUR

There was so short an interval, and so little weeding done, before the second pair appeared, that Cadfael could not choose but reason that the two couples must have met at the corner of his herber, and perhaps exchanged at least a friendly word or two, since they had travelled side by side the last miles of their road here.

The girl walked solicitously beside her brother, giving him the smoothest part of the path, and keeping a hand supportingly under his left elbow, ready to prop him at need, but barely touching. Her face was turned constantly towards him, eager and loving. If he was the tended darling, and she the healthy beast of burden, certainly she had no quarrel with the division. Though just once she did look back over her shoulder, with a different, a more tentative smile. She was neat and plain in her homespun country dress, her hair austerely braided, but her face was vivid and glowing as a rose, and her movements, even at her brother's pace, had a spring and grace to them that spoke of a high and ardent spirit. She was fair for a Welsh girl, her hair a coppery gold, her brows darker, arched hopefully above wide blue eyes. Mistress Weaver could not be far out in supposing that a young man who had hefted this neat little woman out of harm's way in his arms might well remember the experience with pleasure, and not be averse to repeating it. If he could take his eyes from his fellow-pilgrim long enough to attempt it!

The boy came leaning heavily on his crutches, his right leg dangling inertly, turned with the toe twisted inward, and barely brushing the ground. If he could have stood erect he would have been a hand's-breadth taller than his sister, but thus hunched he looked even shorter. Yet the young body was beautifully proportioned, Cadfael judged, watching his approach with a thoughtful eye, wide-shouldered, slim-flanked, the one good leg long, vigorous and shapely. He carried little flesh, indeed he could have done with more, but if he spent his days habitually in pain it was unlikely he had much appetite.

Cadfael's study of him had begun at the twisted foot, and travelling upward, came last to the boy's face. He was fairer than the girl, wheat-gold of hair and brows, his thin, smooth face like ivory, and the eyes that met Cadfael's were a light, brilliant grey-blue, clear as crystal between long, dark lashes. It was a very still and tranquil face, one that had learned patient endurance, and expected to have need of it lifelong. It was clear to Cadfael, in that first exchange of glances, that Rhun did not look for any miraculous deliverance, whatever Mistress Weaver's hopes might be.

'If you please,' said the girl shyly, 'I have brought my brother, as my aunt said I should. And his name is Rhun, and mine is Melangell.'

'She has told me about you,' said Cadfael, beckoning them with him towards his workshop. 'A long journey you've had of it. Come within, and let's make you as easy as we may, while I take a look at this leg of yours. Was there ever an injury brought this on? A fall, or a kick from a horse? Or a bout of the bone-fever?' He settled the boy on the long bench, took the crutches from him and laid them aside, and turned him so that he could stretch out his legs at rest.

The boy, with grave eyes steady on Cadfael's face, slowly shook his head. 'No such accident,' he said in a man's low, clear voice. 'It came, I think, slowly, but I don't remember a time before it. They say I began to falter and fall when I was three or four years old.'

Melangell, hesitant in the doorway—strangely like Ciaran's attendant shadow, thought Cadfael—had her chin on her shoulder now, and turned almost hastily to say: 'Rhun will tell you all his case. He'll be better private with you. I'll come back later, and wait on the seat outside there until you need me.'

Rhun's light, bright eyes, transparent as sunlit ice, smiled at her warmly over Cadfael's shoulder. 'Do go,' he said. 'So fine and sunny a day, you should make good use of it, without me dangling about you.'

She gave him a long, anxious glance, but half her mind was already away; and satisfied that he was in good hands, she made her hasty reverence, and fled. They were left looking at each other, strangers still, and yet in tentative touch.

'She goes to find Matthew,' said Rhun simply, confident of being understood. 'He was good to her. And to me, also—once he carried me the last piece of the way to our night's lodging on his back. She likes him, and he would like her, if he could truly see her, but he seldom sees anyone but Ciaran.'

This blunt simplicity might well get him the reputation of an innocent, though that would be the world's mistake. What he saw, he said— provided, Cadfael hoped, he had already taken the measure of the person to whom he spoke—and he saw more than most, having so much more need to observe and record, to fill up the hours of his day.

'They were here?' asked Rhun, shifting obediently to allow Cadfael to strip down the long hose from his hips and his maimed leg.

'They were here. Yes, I know.'

'I would like her to be happy.'

'She has it in her to be very happy,' said Cadfael, answering in kind, almost without his will. The boy had a quality of dazzle about him that made unstudied answers natural, almost inevitable. There had been, he thought, the slightest of stresses on 'her'. Rhun had little

66

enough expectation that he could ever be happy, but he wanted happiness for his sister. 'Now pay heed,' said Cadfael, bending to his own duties, 'for this is important. Close your eyes, and be at ease as far as you can, and tell me where I find a spot that gives pain. First, thus at rest, is there any pain now?'

Docilely Rhun closed his eyes and waited, breathing softly. 'No, I am quite easy now.'

Good, for all his sinews lay loose and trustful, and at least in that state he felt no pain. Cadfael began to finger his way, at first very gently and soothingly, all down the thigh and calf of the helpless leg, probing and manipulating. Thus stretched out at rest, the twisted limb partially regained its proper alignment, and showed fairly formed, though much wasted by comparison with the left, and marred by the inturned toe and certain tight, bunched knots of sinew in the calf. He sought out these, and let his fingers dig deep there, wrestling with hard tissue.

'There I feel it,' said Rhun, breathing deep. 'It doesn't feel like pain—yes, it hurts, but not for crying. A good hurt . . .'

Brother Cadfael oiled his hands, smoothed a palm over the shrunken calf, and went to work with firm fingertips, working tendons unexercised for years, beyond that tensed touch of toe upon ground. He was gentle and slow, feeling for the hard cores of resistance. There were unnatural tensions there, that

67

would not melt to him yet. He let his fingers work softly, and his mind probe elsewhere.

'You were orphaned early. How long have you been with your Aunt Weaver?'

'Seven years now,' said Rhun almost drowsily, soothed by the circling fingers. 'I know we are a burden to her, but she never says it, nor she would never let any other say it. She has a good business, but small, it provides her needs and keeps two men at work, but she is not rich. Melangell works hard keeping the house and the kitchen, and earns her keep. I have learned to weave, but I am slow at it. I can neither stand for long nor sit for long, I am no profit to her. But she never speaks of it, for all she has an edge to her tongue when she pleases.'

'She would,' agreed Cadfael peacefully. 'A woman with many cares is liable to be short in her speech now and again, and no ill meant. She has brought you here for a miracle. You know that? Why else would you all three have walked all this way, measuring out the stages day by day at your pace? And yet I think you have no expectation of grace. Do you not believe Saint Winifred can do wonders?'

'I?' The boy was startled, he opened great eyes clearer than the clear waters Cadfael had navigated long ago, in the eastern fringes of the Midland Sea, over pale and glittering sand. 'Oh, you mistake me, I *do* believe. But why for me? In case like mine we come by our

68

thousands, in worse case by the hundred. How dare I ask to be among the first? Besides, what I have I can bear. There are some who cannot bear what they have. The saint will know where to choose. There is no reason her choice should fall on me.'

'Then why did you consent to come?' Cadfael asked.

Rhun turned his head aside, and eyelids blue-veined like the petals of anemones veiled his eyes. 'They wished it, I did what they wanted. And there was Melangell . . .'

Yes, Melangell who was altogether comely and bright and a charm to the eye, thought Cadfael. Her brother knew her dowryless, and wished her a little of joy and a decent marriage, and there at home, working hard in house and kitchen, and known for a penniless niece, suitors there were none. A venture so far upon the roads, to mingle with so various a company, might bring forth who could tell what chances?

In moving Rhun had plucked at a nerve that gripped and twisted him, he eased himself back against the timber wall with aching care. Cadfael drew up the homespun hose over the boy's nakedness, knotted him decent, and gently drew down his feet, the sound and the crippled, to the beaten earth floor.

'Come again to me tomorrow, after High Mass, for I think I can help you, if only a little. Now sit until I see if that sister of yours is

69

waiting, and if not, you may rest easy until she comes. And I'll give you a single draught to take this night when you go to your bed. It will ease your pain and help you to sleep.'

The girl was there, still and solitary against the sun-warmed wall, the brightness of her face clouded over, as though some eager expectation had turned into a grey disappointment; but at the sight of Rhun emerging she rose with a resolute smile for him, and her voice was as gay and heartening as ever as they moved slowly away.

*   *   *

He had an opportunity to study all of them next day at High Mass, when doubtless his mind should have been on higher things, but obstinately would not rise above the quivering crest of Mistress Weaver's head-cloth, and the curly dark crown of Matthew's thick crop of hair. Almost all the inhabitants of the guest-halls, the gentles who had separate apartments as well as the male and female pilgrims who shared the two common dortoirs, came in their best to this one office of the day, whatever they did with the rest of it. Mistress Weaver paid devout attention to every word of the office, and several times nudged Melangell sharply in the ribs to recall her to duty, for as often as not her head was turned sidewise, and her gaze directed rather at Matthew than at the altar. No question but her fancy, if not her whole heart, was deeply engaged there. As for Matthew, he stood at Ciaran's shoulder, always within touch. But twice at least he looked round, and his brooding eyes rested, with no change of countenance, upon Melangell. Yet on the one occasion when their glances met, it was Matthew who turned abruptly away.

That young man, thought Cadfael, aware of the broken encounter of eyes, has a thing to do which no girl must be allowed to hinder or spoil: to get his fellow safely to his journey's end at Aberdaron.

He was already a celebrated figure in the enclave, this Ciaran. There was nothing secret about him, he spoke freely and humbly of himself. He had been intended for ordination, but had not yet gone beyond the first step as sub-deacon, and had not reached, and now never would reach, the tonsure. Brother Jerome, always a man to insinuate himself as close as might be to any sign of superlative virtue and holiness, had cultivated and questioned him, and freely retailed what he had learned to any of the brothers who would listen. The story of Ciaran's mortal sickness and penitential pilgrimage home to Aberdaron was known to all. The austerities he practised upon himself made a great impression. Brother Jerome held that the house was honoured in receiving such a man. And indeed that lean, passionate face, burning-eyed beneath the uncropped brown hair, had a vehement force and fervour.

Rhun could not kneel, but stood steady and stoical on his crutches throughout the office, his eyes fixed, wide and bright, upon the altar. In this soft, dim light within, already reflecting from every stone surface the muted brightness of a cloudless day outside, Cadfael saw that the boy was beautiful, the planes of his face as suave and graceful as any girl's, the curving of his fair hair round ears and cheeks angelically pure and chaste. If the woman with no son of her own doted on him, and was willing to forsake her living for a matter of weeks on the off-chance of a miracle that would heal him, who could wonder at her?

Since both his attention and his eyes were straying, Cadfael gave up the struggle and let them stray at large over all those devout heads, gathered in a close assembly and filling the nave of the church. An important pilgrimage has much of the atmosphere of a public fair about it, and brings along with it all the hangers-on who frequent such occasions, the pickpockets, the plausible salesmen of relics, sweetmeats, remedies, the fortune-tellers, the gamblers, the swindlers and cheats of all kinds. And some of these cultivate the most respectable of appearances, and prefer to work from within the pale rather than set up in the Foregate as at a market. It was always worth running an eye over the ranks within, as Hugh's sergeants were certainly doing along the ranks without, to mark down probable sources of trouble before ever the trouble began.

This congregation certainly looked precisely what it purported to be. Nevertheless, there were a few there worth a second glance. Three modest, unobtrusive tradesmen who had arrived closely one after another and rapidly and openly made acquaintance, to all appearances until then strangers: Walter Bagot, glover; John Shure, tailor; William Hales, farrier. Small craftsmen making this their summer holiday, and modestly out to enjoy it. And why not? Except that Cadfael had noted the tailor's hands devoutly folded, and observed that he cultivated the long, well-tended nails of a fairground sharper, hardly suitable for a tailor's work. He made a mental note of their faces, the glover rounded and glossy, as if oiled with the same dressing he used on his leathers, the tailor lean-jowled and sedate, with lank hair curtaining a lugubrious face, the farrier square, brown and twinkling of eye, the picture of honest good-humour.

They might be what they claimed. They might not. Hugh would be on the watch, so would the careful tavern-keepers of the Foregate and the town, by no means eager to hold their doors open to the fleecers and skinners of their own neighbours and customers.

Cadfael went out from Mass with his brethren, very thoughtful, and found Rhun already waiting for him in the herbarium.

*   *   *

The boy sat passive and submitted himself to Cadfael's handling, saying no word beyond his respectful greeting. The rhythm of the questing fingers, patiently coaxing apart the rigid tissues that lamed him, had a soothing effect, even when they probed deeply enough to cause pain. He let his head lean back against the timbers of the wall, and his eyes gradually closed. The tension of his cheeks and lips showed that he was not sleeping, but Cadfael was able to study the boy's face closely as he worked on him, and note his pallor, and the dark rings round his eyes.

'Well, did you take the dose I gave you for the night?' asked Cadfael, guessing at the answer.

'No.' Rhun opened his eyes apprehensively, to see if he was to be reproved for it, but Cadfael's face showed neither surprise nor reproach.

'Why not?'

'I don't know. Suddenly I felt there was no need. I was happy,' said Rhun, his eyes again closed, the better to examine his own actions and motives. 'I had prayed. It's not that I

74

doubt the saint's power. Suddenly it seemed to me that I need not even wish to be healed . . . that I ought to offer up my lameness and pain freely, not as a price for favour. People bring offerings, and I have nothing else to offer. Do you think it might be acceptable? I meant it humbly.'

There could hardly be, thought Cadfael, among all her devotees, a more costly oblation. He has gone far along a difficult road who has come to the point of seeing that deprivation, pain and disability are of no consequence at all, beside the inward conviction of grace, and the secret peace of the soul. An acceptance which can only be made for a man's own self, never for any other. Another's grief is not to be tolerated, if there can be anything done to alleviate it.

'And did you sleep well?'

'No. But it didn't matter. I lay quiet all night long. I tried to bear it gladly. And I was not the only one there wakeful.' He slept in the common dormitory for the men, and there must be several among his fellows there afflicted in one way or another, besides the sick and possibly contagious whom Brother Edmund had isolated in the infirmary. 'Ciaran was restless, too,' said Rhun reflectively. 'When it was all silent, after Lauds, he got up very quietly from his cot, trying not to disturb anyone, and started towards the door. I thought then how strange it was that he took his belt and scrip with him . . .'

Cadfael was listening intently enough by this time. Why, indeed, if a man merely needed relief for his body during the night, should he burden himself with carrying his possessions about with him? Though the habit of being wary of theft, in such shared accommodation, might persist even when half-asleep, and in monastic care into the bargain.

'Did he so, indeed? And what followed?'

'Matthew has his own pallet drawn close beside Ciaran's, even in the night he lies with a hand stretched out to touch. Besides, you know, he seems to know by instinct whatever ails Ciaran. He rose up in an instant, and reached out and took Ciaran by the arm. And Ciaran started and gasped, and blinked round at him, like a man startled awake suddenly, and whispered that he'd been asleep and dreaming, and had dreamed it was time to start out on the road again. So then Matthew took the scrip from him and laid it aside, and they both lay down in their beds again, and all was quiet as before. But I don't think Ciaran slept well, even after that, his dream had disturbed his mind too much, I heard him twisting and turning for a long time.'

'Did they know,' asked Cadfael, 'that you were also awake, and had heard what passed?'

'I can't tell. I made no pretence, and the pain was bad, I think they must have heard me shifting . . . I couldn't help it. But of course I

76

made no sign, it would have been discourteous.'

So it passed as a dream, perhaps for the benefit of Rhun, or any other who might be wakeful as he was. True enough, a sick man troubled by night might very well rise by stealth to leave his friend in peace, out of consideration. But then, if he needed ease, he would have been forced to explain himself and go, when his friend nevertheless started awake to restrain him. Instead, he had pleaded a deluding dream, and lain down again. And men rousing in dreams do move silently, almost as if by stealth. It could be, it must be, simply what it seemed.

'You travelled some miles of the way with those two, Rhun. How did you all fare together on the road? You must have got to know them as well as any here.'

'It was their being slow, like us, that kept us all together, after my sister was nearly ridden down, and Matthew ran and caught her up and leaped the ditch with her. They were just slowly overtaking us then, after that we went on all together for company. But I wouldn't say we got to know them—they are so rapt in each other. And then, Ciaran was in pain, and that kept him silent, though he did tell us where he was bound, and why. It's true Melangell and Matthew took to walking last, behind us, and he carried our few goods for her, having so little of his own to carry. I never

77

wondered at Ciaran being so silent,' said Rhun simply, 'seeing what he had to bear. And my Aunt Alice can talk for two,' he ended guilelessly.

So she could, and no doubt did, all the rest of the way into Shrewsbury.

'That pair, Ciaran and Matthew,' said Cadfael, still delicately probing, 'they never told you how they came together? Whether they were kin, or friends, or had simply met and kept company on the road? For they're much of an age, even of a kind, young men of some schooling, I fancy, bred to clerking or squiring, and yet not kin, or don't acknowledge it, and after their fashion very differently made. A man wonders how they ever came to be embarked together on this journey. It was south of Warwick when you met them? I wonder from how far south they came.'

'They never spoke of such things,' owned Rhun, himself considering them for the first time. 'It was good to have company on the way, one stout young man at least. The roads can be perilous for two women, with only a cripple like me. But now you speak of it, no, we did not learn much of where they came from, or what bound them together. Unless my sister knows more. There were days,' said Rhun, shifting to assist Brother Cadfael's probings into the sinews of his thigh, 'when she and Matthew grew quite easy and talkative behind us.'

Cadfael doubted whether the subject of their conversation then had been anything but their two selves, brushing sleeves pleasurably along the summer highways, she in constant recall of the moment when she was snatched up bodily and swung across the ditch against Matthew's heart, he in constant contemplation of the delectable creature dancing at his elbow, and recollection of the feel of her slight, warm, frightened weight on his breast.

'But he'll hardly look at her now,' said Rhun regretfully. 'He's too intent on Ciaran, and Melangell will come between. But it costs him a dear effort to turn away from her, all the same.'

Cadfael stroked down the misshapen leg, and rose to scrub his oily hands. 'There, that's enough for today. But sit quiet a while and rest before you go. And will you take the draught tonight? At least keep it by you, and do what you feel to be right and best. But remember it's a kindness sometimes to accept help, a kindness to the giver. Would you wilfully inflict torment on yourself as Ciaran does? No, not you, you are too modest by far to set yourself up for braver and more to be worshipped than other men. So never think you do wrong by sparing yourself discomfort. Yet it's your choice, make it as you see fit.'

When the boy took up his crutches again and tapped his way out along the path towards the great court, Cadfael followed him at a distance, to watch his progress without embarrassing him. He could mark no change as yet. The stretched toe still barely dared touch ground, and still turned inward. And yet the sinews, cramped as they were, had some small force in them, instead of being withered and atrophied as he would have expected. If I had him here long enough, he thought, I could bring back some ease and use into that leg. But he'll go as he came. In three days now all will be over, the festival ended for this year, the guest-hall emptying. Ciaran and his guardian shadow will pass on northwards and westwards into Wales, and Dame Weaver will take her chicks back home to Campden. And those two, who might very well have made a fair match if things had been otherwise, will go their separate ways, and never see each other again. It's in the nature of things that those who gather in great numbers for the feasts of the church should also disperse again to their various duties afterwards. Still, they need not all go away unchanged.

CHAPTER FIVE

Brother Adam of Reading, being lodged in the dortoir with the monks of the house, had had leisure to observe his fellow pilgrims of the guest-hall only at the offices of the church, and in their casual comings and goings about the precinct; and it happened that he came from

80

the garden towards mid-afternoon, with Cadfael beside him, just as Ciaran and Matthew were crossing the court towards the cloister garth, there to sit in the sun for an hour or two before Vespers. There were plenty of others, monks, lay servants and guests, busy on their various occasions, but Ciaran's striking figure and painfully slow and careful gait marked him out for notice.

'Those two,' said Brother Adam, halting, 'I have seen before. At Abingdon, where I spent the first night after leaving Reading. They were lodged there the same night.'

'At Abingdon!' Cadfael echoed thoughtfully. 'So they came from far south. You did not cross them again after Abingdon, on the way here?'

'It was not likely. I was mounted. And then, I had my abbot's mission to Leominster, which took me out of the direct way. No, I saw no more of them, never until now. But they can hardly be mistaken, once seen.'

'In what sort of case were they at Abingdon?' asked Cadfael, his eyes following the two inseparable figures until they vanished into the cloister. 'Would you say they had been long on the road before that night's halt? The man is pledged to go barefoot to Aberdaron, it would not take many miles to leave the mark on him.'

'He was going somewhat lamely, even then. They had both the dust of the roads on them.

It might have been their first day's walking that ended there, but I doubt it.'

'He came to me to have his feet tended, yesterday,' said Cadfael, 'and I must see him again before evening. Two or three days of rest will set him up for the next stage of his walk.' From more than a day's going south of Abingdon to the remotest tip of Wales, a long, long walk. 'A strange, even a mistaken, piety it seems to me, to take upon oneself ostentatious pains, when there are poor fellows enough in the world who are born to pain they have not chosen, and carry it with humility.'

'The simple believe it brings merit,' said Brother Adam tolerantly. 'It may be he has no other claim upon outstanding virtue, and clutches at this.'

'But he's no simple soul,' said Cadfael with conviction, 'whatever he may be. He has, he tells me, a mortal disease, and is going to end his days in blessedness and peace at Aberdaron, and have his bones laid in Ynys Enlli, which is a noble ambition in a man of Welsh blood. The voluntary assumption of pain beyond his doom may even be a pennon of defiance, a wag of the hand against death. That I could understand. But I would not approve it.'

'It's very natural you should frown on it,' agreed Adam, smiling indulgence upon his companion and himself alike, 'seeing you are schooled to the alleviation of pain, and feel it

82

to be a violator and an enemy. By the very virtue of these plants we have learned to use.' He patted the leather scrip at his girdle, and the soft rustle of seeds within answered him. They had been sorting over Cadfael's day saucers of new seed from this freshly ripening year, and he had helped himself to two or three not native in his own herbarium. 'It is as good a dragon to fight as any in this world, pain.'

They had gone some yards more towards the stone steps that led up to the main door of the guest-hall, in no hurry, and taking pleasure in the contemplation of so much bustle and motion, when Brother Adam checked abruptly and stood at gaze.

'Well, well, I think you may have got some of our southern sinners, as well as our would-be saints!'

Cadfael, surprised, followed where Adam was gazing, and stood to hear what further he would have to say, for the individual in question was the least remarkable of men at first glance. He stood close to the gatehouse, one of a small group constantly on hand there to watch the new arrivals and the general commerce of the day. A big man, but so neatly and squarely built that his size was not wholly apparent, he stood with his thumbs in the belt of his plain but ample gown, which was nicely cut and fashioned to show him no nobleman, and no commoner, either, but a solid, respectable, comfortably provided fellow of the middle kind, merchant or tradesman. One of those who form the backbone of many a township in England, and can afford the occasional pilgrimage by way of a well-earned holiday. He gazed benignly upon the activity around him from a plump, shrewd, well-shaven face, favouring the whole creation with a broad, contented smile.

'That,' said Cadfael, eyeing his companion with bright enquiry, 'is, or so I am informed, one Simeon Poer, a merchant of Guildford, come on pilgrimage for his soul's sake, and because the summer chances to be very fine and inviting. And why not? Do you know of a reason?'

'Simeon Poer may well be his name,' said Brother Adam, 'or he may have half a dozen more ready to trot forward at need. I never knew a name for him, but his face and form I do know. Father Abbot uses me a good deal on his business outside the cloister and I have occasion to know most of the fairs and markets in our shire and beyond. I've seen that fellow—not gowned like a provost, as he is now, I grant you, but by the look of him he's been doing well lately—round every fairground, cultivating the company of those young, green roisterers who frequent every such gathering. For the contents of their pockets, surely. Most likely, dice. Even more likely, loaded dice. Though I wouldn't say he

84

might not pick a pocket here and there, if business was bad. A quicker means to the same end, if a riskier.'

So knowing and practical a brother Cadfael had not encountered for some years among the innocents. Plainly Brother Adam's frequent sallies out of the cloister on the abbot's business had broadened his horizons. Cadfael regarded him with respect and warmth, and turned to study the smiling, benevolent merchant more closely.

'You're sure of him?'

'Sure that he's the same man, yes. Sure enough of his practices to challenge him openly, no, hardly, since he has never yet been taken up but once, and then he proved so slippery he slithered through the bailiff's fingers. But keep a weather eye on him, and this may be where he'll make the slip every rogue makes in the end, and get his comeuppance.'

'If you're right,' said Cadfael, 'has he not strayed rather far from his own haunts? In my experience, from years back I own, his kind seldom left the region where they knew their way about better than the bailiffs. Has he made the south country so hot for him that he must run for a fresh territory? That argues something worse than cheating at dice.'

Brother Adam hoisted dubious shoulders. 'It could be. Some of our scum have found the disorders of faction very profitable, in their own way, just as their lords and masters have in theirs. Battles are not for them—far too dangerous to their own skins. But the brawls that blow up in towns where uneasy factions come together are meat and drink to them. Pockets to be picked, riots to be started—discreetly from the rear—unoffending elders who look prosperous to be knocked on the head or knifed from behind or have their purse-strings cut in the confusion . . . Safer and easier than taking to the woods and living wild for prey, as their kind do in the country.'

Just such gatherings, thought Cadfael, as that at Winchester, where at least one man was knifed in the back and left dying. Might not the law in the south be searching for this man, to drive him so far from his usual hunting-grounds? For some worse offence than cheating silly young men of their money at dice? Something as black as murder itself?

'There are two or three others in the common guest-hall,' he said, 'about whom I have my doubts, but this man has had no truck with them so far as I've seen. But I'll bear it in mind, and keep a watchful eye open, and have Brother Denis do the same. And I'll mention what you say to Hugh Beringar, too, before this evening's out. Both he and the town provost will be glad to have fair warning.'

*   *   *

86

Since Ciaran was sitting quietly in the cloister garth, it seemed a pity he should be made to walk through the gardens to the herbarium, when Cadfael's broad brown feet were in excellent condition, and sensibly equipped with stout sandals. So Cadfael fetched the salve he had used on Ciaran's wounds and bruises, and the spirit that would brace and toughen his tender soles, and brought them to the cloister. It was pleasant there in the afternoon sun, and the turf was thick and springy and cool to bare feet. The roses were coming into full bloom, and their scent hung in the warm air like a benediction. But two such closed and sunless faces! Was the one truly condemned to an early death, and the other to lose and mourn so close a friend?

Ciaran was speaking as Cadfael approached, and did not at first notice him, but even when he was aware of the visitor bearing down on them he continued steadily to the end, ' . . . you do but waste your time, for it will not happen. Nothing will be changed, don't look for it. Never! You might far better leave me and go home.'

Did the one of them believe in Saint Winifred's power, and pray and hope for a miracle? And was the other, the sick man, all too passionately of Rhun's mind, and set on offering his early death as an acceptable and willing sacrifice, rather than ask for healing?

Matthew had not yet noticed Cadfael's

approach. His deep voice, measured and resolute, said just audibly, 'Save your breath! For I will go with you, step for step, to the very end.'

Then Cadfael was close, and they were both aware of him, and stirred defensively out of their private anguish, heaving in breath and schooling their faces to confront the outer world decently. They drew a little apart on the stone bench, welcoming Cadfael with somewhat strained smiles.

'I saw no need to make you come to me,' said Cadfael, dropping to his knees and opening his scrip in the bright green turf, 'when I am better able to come to you. So sit and be easy, and let me see how much work is yet to be done before you can go forth in good heart.'

'This is kind, brother,' said Ciaran, rousing himself with a sigh. 'Be assured that I do go in good heart, for my pilgrimage is short and my arrival assured.'

At the other end of the bench Matthew's voice said softly, 'Amen!'

After that it was all silence as Cadfael anointed the swollen soles, kneading spirit vigorously into the misused skin, surely heretofore accustomed always to going well shod, and soothed the ointment of cleavers into the healing grazes.

'There! Keep off your feet through tomorrow, but for such offices as you feel you must attend. Here there's no need to go far.

And I'll come to you tomorrow and have you fit to stand somewhat longer the next day, when the saint is brought home.' When he spoke of her now, he hardly knew whether he was truly speaking of the mortal substance of Saint Winifred, which was generally believed to be in that silver-chaced reliquary, or of some hopeful distillation of her spirit which could fill with sanctity even an empty coffin, even a casket containing pitiful, faulty human bones, unworthy of her charity, but subject, like all mortality, to the capricious, smiling mercies of those above and beyond question. If you could reason by pure logic for the occurrence of miracles, they would not be miracles, would they?

He scrubbed his hands on a handful of wool, and rose from his knees. In some twenty minutes or so it would be time for Vespers.

He had taken his leave, and almost reached the archway into the great court, when he heard rapid steps at his heels, a hand reached deprecatingly for his sleeve, and Matthew's voice said in his ear, 'Brother Cadfael, you left this lying.'

It was his jar of ointment, of rough, greenish pottery, almost invisible in the grass. The young man held it out in the palm of a broad, strong, workmanlike hand, long-fingered and elegant. Dark eyes, reserved but earnestly curious, searched Cadfael's face.

Cadfael took the jar with thanks, and put it

away in his scrip. Ciaran sat where Matthew had left him, his face and burning gaze turned towards them; they stood at a distance, between him and the outer day, and he had, for one moment, the look of a soul abandoned to absolute solitude in a populous world.

Cadfael and Matthew stood gazing in speculation and uncertainty into each other's eyes. This was that able, ready young man who had leaped into action at need, upon whom Melangell had fixed her young, unpractised heart, and to whom Rhun had surely looked for a hopeful way out for his sister, whatever might become of himself. Good, cultivated stock, surely, bred of some small gentry and taught a little Latin as well as his schooling in arms. How, except by the compulsion of inordinate love, did this one come to be ranging the country like a penniless vagabond, without root or attachment but to a dying man?

'Tell me truth,' said Cadfael. 'Is it indeed true—is it *certain*—that Ciaran goes this way towards his death?'

There was a brief moment of silence, as Matthew's wide-set eyes grew larger and darker. Then he said very softly and deliberately, 'It is truth. He is already marked for death. Unless your saint has a miracle for us, there is nothing can save him. Or me!' he ended abruptly, and wrenched himself away to return to his devoted watch.

90

*   *   *

Cadfael turned his back on supper in the refectory, and set off instead along the Foregate towards the town. Over the bridge that spanned the Severn, in through the gate, and up the curving slope of the Wyle to Hugh Beringar's town house. There he sat and nursed his godson Giles, a large, comely, self-willed child, fair like his mother, and long of limb, some day to dwarf his small, dark, sardonic father. Aline brought food and wine for her husband and his friend, and then sat down to her needlework, favouring her menfolk from time to time with a smiling glance of serene contentment. When her son fell asleep in Cadfael's lap she rose and lifted the boy away gently. He was heavy for her, but she had learned how to carry him lightly balanced on arm and shoulder. Cadfael watched her fondly as she bore the child away into the next room to his bed, and closed the door between.

'How is it possible that that girl can grow every day more radiant and lovely? I've known marriage rub the fine bloom off many a handsome maid. Yet it suits her as a halo does a saint.'

'Oh, there's something to be said for marriage,' said Hugh idly. 'Do I look so poorly on it? Though it's an odd study for a man of your habit, after all these years of celibacy . . .

And all the stravagings about the world before that! You can't have thought too highly of the wedded state, or you'd have ventured on it yourself. You took no vows until past forty, and you a well-set-up young fellow crusading all about the east with the best of them. How do I know you have not an Aline of your own locked away somewhere, somewhere in your remembrance, as dear as mine is to me? Perhaps even a Giles of your own,' he added, whimsically smiling, 'a Giles God knows where, grown a man now . . .'

Cadfael's silence and stillness, though perfectly easy and complacent, nevertheless sounded a mute warning in Hugh's perceptive senses. On the edge of drowsiness among his cushions after a long day out of doors, he opened a black, considering eye to train upon his friend's musing face, and withdrew delicately into practical business.

'Well, so this Simeon Poer is known in the south. I'm grateful to you and to Brother Adam for the nudge, though so far the man has set no foot wrong here. But these others you've pictured for me . . . At Wat's tavern in the Foregate they've had practice in marking down strangers who come with a fair or a feast, and spread themselves large about the town. Wat tells my people he has a group moving in, very merry, some of them strangers. They could well be these you name. Some of them, of course, the usual young fellows of the town and the Foregate with more pence than sense. They've been drinking a great deal, and throwing dice. Wat does not like the way the dice fall.'

'It's as I supposed,' said Cadfael, nodding. 'For every Mass of ours they'll be celebrating the Gamblers' Mass elsewhere. And by all means let the fools throw their money after their sense, so the odds be fair. But Wat knows a loaded throw when he sees one.'

'He knows how to rid his house of the plague, too. He has hissed in the ears of one of the strangers that his tavern is watched, and they'd be wise to take their school out of there. And for tonight he has a lad on the watch, to find out where they'll meet. Tomorrow night we'll have at them, and rid you of them in good time for the feast day, if all goes well.'

*   *   *

Which would be a very welcome cleansing, thought Cadfael, making his way back across the bridge in the first limpid dusk, with the river swirling its coiled currents beneath him in gleams of reflected light, low summer water leaving the islands outlined in swathes of drowned, browning weed. But as yet there was nothing to shed light, even by reflected, phantom gleams, upon that death so far away in the south country, whence the merchant Simeon Poer had set out. On pilgrimage for his respectable soul? Or in flight from a law aroused too fiercely for his safety, by something graver than the cozening of fools? Though Cadfael felt too close to folly himself to be loftily complacent even about that, however much it might be argued that gamblers deserved all they got.

The great gate of the abbey was closed, but the wicket in it stood open, shedding sunset light through from the west. In the mild dazzle Cadfael brushed shoulders and sleeves with another entering, and was a little surprised to be hoisted deferentially through the wicket by a firm hand at his elbow.

'Give you goodnight, brother!' sang a mellow voice in his ear, as the returning guest stepped within on his heels. And the solid, powerful, woollen-gowned form of Simeon Poer, self-styled merchant of Guildford, rolled vigorously past him, and crossed the great court to the stone steps of the guest-hall.

CHAPTER SIX

They were emerging from High Mass on the morning of the twenty-first day of June, the eve of Saint Winifred's translation, stepping out into a radiant morning, when the abbot's sedate progress towards his lodging was rudely disrupted by a sudden howl of dismay among

94

the dispersing multitude of worshippers, a wild ripple of movement cleaving a path through their ranks, and the emergence of a frantic figure lurching forth on clumsy, naked feet to clutch at the abbot's robe, and appeal in a loud, indignant cry, 'Father Abbot, stand my friend and give me justice, for I am robbed! A thief, there is a thief among us!'

The abbot looked down in astonishment and concern into the face of Ciaran, convulsed and ablaze with resentment and distress.

'Father, I beg you, see justice done! I am helpless unless you help me!'

He awoke, somewhat late, to the unwarranted violence of his behaviour, and fell on his knees at the abbot's feet. 'Pardon, pardon! I am too loud and troublous, I hardly know what I say!'

The press of gossiping, festive worshippers just loosed from Mass had fallen quiet all in a moment, and instead of dispersing drew in about them to listen and stare, avidly curious. The monks of the house, hindered in their orderly departure, hovered in quiet deprecation. Cadfael looked beyond the kneeling, imploring figure of Ciaran for its inseparable twin, and found Matthew just shouldering his way forward out of the crowd, open-mouthed and wide-eyed in patent bewilderment, to stand at gaze a few paces apart, and frown helplessly from the abbot to Ciaran and back again, in search of the cause of this abrupt turmoil. Was it possible that something had happened to the one that the other of the matched pair did not know?

'Get up!' said Radulfus, erect and calm. 'No need to kneel. Speak out whatever you have to say, and you shall have right.'

The pervasive silence spread, grew, filled even the most distant reaches of the great court. Those who had already scattered to the far corners turned and crept unobtrusively back again, large-eyed and prick-eared, to hang upon the fringes of the crowd already assembled.

Ciaran clambered to his feet, voluble before he was erect. 'Father, I had a ring, the copy of one the lord bishop of Winchester keeps for his occasions, bearing his device and inscription. Such copies he uses to afford safe-conduct to those he sends forth on his business or with his blessing, to open doors to them and provide protection on the road. Father, the ring is gone!'

'This ring was given to you by Henry of Blois himself?' asked Radulfus.

'No, Father, not in person. I was in the service of the prior of Hyde Abbey, a lay clerk, when this mortal sickness came on me, and I took this vow of mine to spend my remaining days in the canonry of Aberdaron. My prior— you know that Hyde is without an abbot, and has been for some years—my prior asked the lord bishop, of his goodness, to give me what protection he could for my journey . . .'

So that had been the starting point of this barefoot journey, thought Cadfael, enlightened. Winchester itself, or as near as made no matter, for the New Minster of that city, always a jealous rival of the Old, where Bishop Henry presided, had been forced to abandon its old home in the city thirty years ago, and banished to Hyde Mead, on the north-western outskirts. There was no love lost between Henry and the community at Hyde, for it was the bishop who had been instrumental in keeping them deprived of an abbot for so long, in pursuit of his own ambition of turning them into an episcopal monastery. The struggle had been going on for some time, the bishop deploying various schemes to get the house into his own hands, and the prior using every means to resist these manipulations. It seemed Henry had still the grace to show compassion even on a servant of the hostile house, when he fell under the threat of disease and death. The traveller over whom the bishop-legate spread his protecting hand would pass unmolested wherever law retained its validity. Only those irreclaimably outlaw already would dare interfere with him.

'Father, the ring is gone, stolen from me this very morning. See here, the slashed threads that held it!' Ciaran heaved forward the drab linen scrip that rode at his belt, and showed two dangling ends of cord, very cleanly severed. 'A sharp knife—someone here has such a dagger. And my ring is gone!'

Prior Robert was at the abbot's elbow by then, agitated out of his silvery composure. 'Father, what this man says is true. He showed me the ring. Given to ensure him aid and hospitality on his journey, which is of most sad and solemn import. If now it is lost, should not the gate be closed while we enquire?'

'Let it be so,' said Radulfus, and stood silent to see Brother Jerome, ever ready and assiduous on the prior's heels, run to see the order carried out. 'Now, take breath and thought, for your loss cannot be lost far. You did not wear the ring, then, but carried it knotted securely by this cord, within your scrip?'

'Yes, Father. It was beyond words precious to me.'

'And when did you last ascertain that it was still there, and safe?'

'Father, this very morning I know I had it. Such few things as I possess, here they lie before you. Could I fail to see if this cord had been cut in the night while I slept? It is not so. This morning all was as I left it last night. I have been bidden to rest, by reason of my barefoot vow. Today I ventured out only for Mass. Here in the very church, in this great press of worshippers, some malevolent has broken every ban, and slashed loose my ring from me.'

And indeed, thought Cadfael, running a considering eye round all the curious, watching faces, it would not be difficult, in such a press, to find the strings that anchored the hidden ring, flick it out from its hiding-place, cut the strings and make away with it, discreetly between crowding bodies, and never be seen by a soul or felt by the victim. A neat thing, done so privately and expertly that even Matthew, who missed nothing that touched his friend, had missed this impudent assault. For Matthew stood there staring, obviously taken by surprise, and unsure as yet how to take this turn of events. His face was unreadable, closed and still, his eyes narrowed and bright, darting from face to face as Ciaran or abbot or prior spoke. Cadfael noted that Melangell had stolen forward close to him, and taken him hesitantly by the sleeve. He did not shake her off. By the slight lift of his head and widening of his eyes he knew who had touched him, and he let his hand feel for hers and clasp it, while his whole attention seemed to be fixed on Ciaran. Somewhere not far behind them Rhun leaned on his crutches, his fair face frowning in anxious dismay, Aunt Alice attendant at his shoulder, bright with curiosity. Here are we all, thought Cadfael, and not one of us knows what is in any other mind, or who has done what has been done, or what will come of it for any of those who look on and marvel.

'You cannot tell,' suggested Prior Robert,

agitated and grieved, 'who stood close to you during the service? If indeed some ill-conditioned person has so misused the holy office as to commit theft in the very sacredness of the Mass . . .'

'Father, I was intent only upon the altar.' Ciaran shook with fervour, holding the ravished scrip open before him with his sparse possessions bared to be seen. 'We were close pressed, so many people . . . as is only seemly, in such a shrine . . . Matthew was close at my back, but so he ever is. Who else there may have been by me, how can I say? There was no man nor woman among us who was not hemmed in every way.'

'It is truth,' said Prior Robert, who had been much gratified at the large attendance. 'Father, the gate is now closed, we are all here who were present at Mass. And surely we all have a desire to see this wrong righted.'

'All, as I suppose,' said Radulfus drily, 'but one. One, who brought in here a knife or dagger sharp enough to slice through these tough cords cleanly. What other intents he brought in with him, I bid him consider and tremble for his soul. Robert, this ring must be found. All men of goodwill here will offer their aid, and show freely what they have. So will every guest who has not theft and sacrilege to hide. And see to it also that enquiry be made, whether other articles of value have not been missed. For one theft means one thief, here within.'

'It shall be seen to, Father,' said Robert fervently. 'No honest, devout pilgrim will grudge to offer his aid. How could he wish to share his lodging here with a thief?'

There was a stir of agreement and support, perhaps slightly delayed, as every man and woman eyed a neighbour, and then in haste elected to speak first. They came from every direction, hitherto unknown to one another, mingling and forming friendships now with the abandon of holiday. But how did they know who was immaculate and who was suspect, now the world had probed a merciless finger within the fold?

'Father,' pleaded Ciaran, still sweating and shaking with distress, 'here I offer in this scrip all that I brought into this enclave. Examine it, show that I have indeed been robbed. Here I came without even shoes to my feet, my all is here in your hands. And my fellow Matthew will open to you his own scrip as freely, an example to all these others that they may deliver themselves pure of blame. What we offer, they will not refuse.'

Matthew had withdrawn his hand from Melangell's sharply at this word. He shifted the unbleached cloth scrip, very like Ciaran's, round upon his hip. Ciaran's meagre travelling equipment lay open in the prior's hands. Robert slid them back into the pouch from which they had come, and looked where

Ciaran's distressed gaze guided him.

'Into your hands, Father, and willingly,' said Matthew, and stripped the bag from its buckles and held it forth.

Robert acknowledged the offering with a grave bow, and opened and probed it with delicate consideration. Most of what was there within he did not display, though he handled it. A spare shirt and linen drawers, crumpled from being carried so, and laundered on the way, probably more than once. The means of a gentleman's sparse toilet, razor, morsel of lye soap, a leather-bound breviary, a lean purse, a folded trophy of embroidered ribbon. Robert drew forth the only item he felt he must show, a sheathed dagger, such as any gentleman might carry at his right hip, barely longer than a man's hand.

'Yes, that is mine,' said Matthew, looking Abbot Radulfus straightly in the eyes. 'It has not slashed through those cords. Nor has it left my scrip since I entered your enclave, Father Abbot.'

Radulfus looked from the dagger to its owner, and briefly nodded. 'I well understand that no young man would set forth on these highroads today without the means of defending himself. All the more if he had another to defend, who carried no weapons. As I understand is your condition, my son. Yet within these walls you should not bear arms.'

'What, then, should I have done?'

demanded Matthew, with a stiffening neck, and a note in his voice that just fell short of defiance.

'What you must do now,' said Radulfus firmly. 'Give it into the care of Brother Porter at the gatehouse, as others have done with their weapons. When you leave here you may reclaim it freely.'

There was nothing to be done but bow the head and give way gracefully, and Matthew managed it decently enough, but not gladly. 'I will do so, Father, and pray your pardon that I did not ask advice before.'

'But, Father,' Ciaran pleaded anxiously, 'my ring ... How shall I survive the way if I have not that safe-conduct to show?'

'Your ring shall be sought throughout this enclave, and every man who bears no guilt for its loss,' said the abbot, raising his voice to carry to the distant fringes of the silent crowd, 'will freely offer his own possessions for inspection. See to it, Robert!'

With that he proceeded on his way, and the crowd, after some moments of stillness as they watched him out of sight, dispersed in a sudden murmur of excited speculation. Prior Robert took Ciaran under his wing, and swept away with him towards the guest-hall, to recruit help from Brother Denis in his enquiries after the bishop's ring; and Matthew, not without one hesitant glance at Melangell, turned on his heel and went hastily after them.

A more innocent and co-operative company than the guests at Shrewsbury abbey that day it would have been impossible to find. Every man opened his bundle or box almost eagerly, in haste to demonstrate his immaculate virtue. The quest, conducted as delicately as possible, went on all the afternoon, but they found no trace of the ring. Moreover, one or two of the better-off inhabitants of the common dormitory, who had had no occasion to penetrate to the bottom of their baggage so far, made grievous discoveries when they were obliged to do so. A yeoman from Lichfield found his reserve purse lighter by half than when he had tucked it away. Master Simeon Poer, one of the first to fling open his possessions, and the loudest in condemning so blasphemous a crime, claimed to have been robbed of a silver chain he had intended to present at the altar next day. A poor parish priest, making this pilgrimage the one fulfilled dream of his life, was left lamenting the loss of a small casket, made by his own hands over more than a year, and decorated with inlays of silver and glass, in which he had hoped to carry back with him some memento of his visit, a dried flower from the garden, even a thread or two drawn from the fringe of the altar-cloth under Saint Winifred's reliquary. A merchant from Worcester could not find his good leather belt to his best coat, saved up for the morrow. One or two others had a suspicion that their belongings had been fingered and scorned, which was worst of all.

It was all over, and fruitless, when Cadfael at last repaired to his workshop in time to await the coming of Rhun. The boy came prompt to his hour, great-eyed and thoughtful, and lay submissive and mute under Cadfael's ministrations, which probed every day a little deeper into his knotted and stubborn tissues.

'Brother,' he said at length, looking up, 'you did not find a dagger in any other man's pouch, did you?'

'No, no such thing.' Though there had been, understandably, a number of small, homely knives, the kind a man needs to hack his bread and meat in lodgings along the way, or meals under a hedge. Many of them were sharp enough for most everyday purposes, but not sharp enough to leave stout cords sheared through without a twitch to betray the assault. 'But men who go shaven carry razors, too, and a blunt razor would be an abomination. Once a thief comes into the pale, child, it's hard for honest men to be a match for him. He who has no scruple has always the advantage of those who keep to rule. But you need not trouble your heart, you've done no wrong to any man. Never let this ill thing spoil tomorrow for you.'

'No,' agreed the boy, still preoccupied. 'But,

105

brother, there *is* another dagger—one, at least. Sheath and all, a good length—I know, I was pressed close against him yesterday at Mass. You know I have to hold fast by my crutches to stand for long, and he had a big linen scrip on his belt, hard against my hand and arm, where we were crowded together. I felt the shape of it, cross-hilt and all. I know! But you did not find it.'

'And who was it,' asked Cadfael, still carefully working the tissues that resisted his fingers, 'who had this armoury about him at Mass?'

'It was that big merchant with the good gown—made from valley wool. I've learned to know cloth. They call him Simeon Poer. But you didn't find it. Perhaps he's handed it to Brother Porter, just as Matthew has had to do now.'

'Perhaps,' said Cadfael. 'When was it you discovered this? Yesterday? And what of today? Was he again close to you?'

'No, not today.'

No, today he had stood stolidly to watch the play, eyes and ears alert, ready to open his pouch there before all if need be, smiling complacently as the abbot directed the disarming of another man. He had certainly had no dagger on him then, however he had disposed of it in the meantime. There were hiding-places enough here within the walls, for a dagger and any amount of small, stolen valuables. To search was itself only a pretence, unless authority was prepared to keep the gates closed and the guests prisoned within until every yard of the gardens had been dug up, and every bed and bench in dortoir and hall pulled to pieces. The sinners have always the start of the honest men.

'It was not fair that Matthew should be made to surrender his dagger,' said Rhun, 'when another man had one still about him. And Ciaran already so terribly afraid to stir, not having his ring. He won't even come out of the dortoir until tomorrow. He is sick for loss of it.'

Yes, that seemed to be true. And how strange, thought Cadfael, pricked into realisation, to see a man sweating for fear, who has already calmly declared himself as one condemned to death? Then why fear? Fear should be dead.

Yet men are strange, he thought in revulsion. And a blessed and quiet death in Aberdaron, well-prepared, and surrounded by the prayers and compassion of like-minded votaries, may well seem a very different matter from crude slaughter by strangers and footpads somewhere in the wilder stretches of the road.

But this Simeon Poer—say he had such a dagger yesterday, and therefore may well have had it on him today, in the crowded array of the Mass. Then what did he do with it so quickly, before Ciaran discovered his loss? And how did he know he must perforce dispose of it quickly? Who had such fair warning of the need, if not the thief?

'Trouble your head no more,' said Cadfael, looking down at the boy's beautiful, vulnerable face, 'for Matthew nor for Ciaran, but think only of the morrow, when you approach the saint. Both she and God see you all, and have no need to be told of what your needs are. All you have to do is wait in quiet for whatever will be. For whatever it may be, it will not be wanton. Did you take your dose last night?'

Rhun's pale, brilliant eyes were startled wide open, sunlight and ice, blindingly clear. 'No. It was a good day, I wanted to give thanks. It isn't that I don't value what you can do for me. Only I wished also to give something. And I did sleep, truly I slept well . . .'

'So do tonight also,' said Cadfael gently, and slid an arm round the boy's body to hoist him steadily upright. 'Say your prayers, think quietly what you should do, do it, and sleep. There is no man living, neither king nor emperor, can do more or better, or trust in a better harvest.'

*   *   *

Ciaran did not stir from within the guest-hall again that day. Matthew did, against all precedent emerging from the arched doorway without his companion, and standing at the head of the stone staircase to the great court with hands spread to touch the courses of the deep doorway, and head drawn back to heave in great breaths of evening air. Supper was eaten, the milder evening stir of movement threaded the court, in the cool, grateful lull before Compline.

Brother Cadfael had left the chapter house before the end of the readings, having a few things to attend to in the herbarium, and was crossing towards the garden when he caught sight of the young man standing there at the top of the steps, breathing in deeply and with evident pleasure. For some reason Matthew looked taller for being alone, and younger, his face closed but tranquil in the soft evening light. When he moved forward and began to descend to the court, Cadfael looked instinctively for the other figure that should have been close behind him, if not in its usual place a step before him, but no Ciaran emerged. Well, he had been urged to rest, and presumably was glad to comply, but never before had Matthew left his side, by night or day, resting or stirring. Not even to follow Melangell, except broodingly with his eyes and against his will.

People, thought Cadfael, going on his way without haste, people are endlessly mysterious, and I am endlessly curious. A sin to be confessed, no doubt, and well worth a penance. As long as man is curious about his fellowman, that appetite alone will keep him alive. Why do folk do the things they do? Why, if you know you are diseased and dying, and wish to reach a desired haven before the end, why do you condemn yourself to do the long journey barefoot, and burden yourself with a weight about your neck? How are you thus rendered more acceptable to God, when you might have lent a hand to someone on the road crippled not by perversity but from birth, like the boy Rhun? And why do you dedicate your youth and strength to following another man step by step the length of the land, and why does he suffer you to be his shadow, when he should be composing his mind to peace, and taking a decent leave of his friends, not laying his own load upon them?

There he checked, rounding the corner of the yew hedge into the rose garden. It was not his fellow-man he beheld, sitting in the turf on the far side of the flower beds, gazing across the slope of the pease-fields beyond and the low, stony, silvery summer waters of the Meole brook, but his fellow-woman, solitary and still, her knees drawn up under her chin and encircled closely by her folded arms. Aunt Alice Weaver, no doubt, was deep in talk with half a dozen worthy matrons of her own generation, and Rhun, surely, already in his bed. Melangell had stolen away alone to be quiet here in the garden and nurse her lame dreams and indomitable hopes. She was a small, dark shape, gold-haloed against the bright west. By the look of that sky tomorrow, Saint Winifred's day, would again be cloudless and beautiful.

The whole width of the rose garden was between them, and she did not hear him come and pass by on the grassy path to his final duties of the day in his workshop, seeing everything put away tidily, checking the stoppers of all his flagons and flasks, and making sure the brazier, which had been in service earlier, was safely quenched and cooled. Brother Oswin, young, enthusiastic and devoted, was nonetheless liable to overlook details, though he had now outlived his tendency to break things. Cadfael ran an eye over everything, and found it good. There was no hurry now, he had time before Compline to sit down here in the wood-scented dimness and think. Time for others to lose and find one another, and use or waste these closing moments of the day. For those three blameless tradesmen, Walter Bagot, glover; John Shure, tailor; William Hales, farrier; to betake themselves to wherever their dice school was to meet this night, and run their necks into Hugh's trap. Time for that more ambiguous character, Simeon Poer, to evade or trip into the same snare, or go the other way about some other nocturnal

111

business of his own. Cadfael had seen two of the former three go out from the gatehouse, and the third follow some minutes later, and was sure in his own mind that the self-styled merchant of Guildford would not be long after them. Time, too, for that unaccountably solitary young man, somehow loosed off his chain, to range this whole territory suddenly opened to him, and happen upon the solitary girl.

Cadfael put up his feet on the wooden bench, and closed his eyes for a brief respite.

*　　　*　　　*

Matthew was there at her back before she knew it. The sudden rustle as he stepped into sun-dried long grass at the edge of the field startled her, and she swung round in alarm, scrambling to her knees and staring up into his face with dilated eyes, half-blinded by the blaze of the sunset into which she had been steadily staring. Her face was utterly open, vulnerable and childlike. She looked as she had looked when he had swept her up in his arms and leaped the ditch with her, clear of the galloping horses. Just so she had opened her eyes and looked up at him, still dazed and frightened, and just so had her fear melted away into wonder and pleasure, finding in him nothing but reassurance, kindness and admiration.

112

That pure, paired encounter of eyes did not last long. She blinked, and shook her head a little to clear her dazzled vision, and looked beyond him, searching, not believing he could be here alone.

'Ciaran . . . ? Is there something you need for him?'

'No,' said Matthew shortly, and for a moment turned his head away. 'He's in his bed.'

'But you never leave his bed!' It was said in innocence, even in anxiety. Whatever she grudged to Ciaran, she still pitied and understood him.

'You see I have left it,' said Matthew harshly. 'I have needs, too . . . a breath of air. And he is very well where he is, and won't stir.'

'I was well sure,' she said with resigned bitterness, 'that you had not come out to look for me.' She made to rise, swiftly and gracefully enough, but he put out a hand, almost against his will, as it seemed, to take her under the wrist and lift her. It was withdrawn as abruptly when she evaded his touch, and rose to her feet unaided. 'But at least,' she said deliberately, 'you did not turn and run from me when you found me. I should be grateful even for that.'

'I am not free,' he protested, stung. 'You know it better than any.'

'Then neither were you free when we kept pace along the road,' said Melangell fiercely,

113

'when you carried my burden, and walked beside me, and let Ciaran hobble along before, where he could not see how you smiled on me then and were gallant and cherished me when the road was rough, and spoke softly, as if you took delight in being beside me. Why did you not give me warning then that you were not free? Or better, take him some other way, and leave us alone? Then I might have taken good heed in time, and in time forgotten you. As now I never shall! Never, to my life's end!'

All the flesh of his lips and cheeks shrank and tightened before her eyes, in a contortion of either rage or pain, she could not tell which. She was staring too close and too passionately to see very clearly. He turned his head sharply away, to evade her eyes.

'You charge me justly,' he said in a harsh whisper, 'I was at fault. I never should have believed there could be so clean and sweet a happiness for me. I should have left you, but I could not . . . Oh, God! You think I could have turned him? He clung to you, to your good aunt . . . Yet I should have been strong enough to hold off from you and let you alone . . .' As rapidly as he had swung away from her he swung back again, reaching a hand to take her by the chin and hold her face to face with him, so ungently that she felt the pressure of his fingers bruising her flesh. 'Do you know how hard a thing you are asking? No! This countenance you never saw, did you, never but

114

through someone else's eyes. Who would provide you a mirror to see yourself? Some pool, perhaps, if ever you had the leisure to lean over and look. How should you know what this face can do to a man already lost? And you marvel I took what I could get for water in a drought, when it walked beside me? I should rather have died than stay beside you, to trouble your peace. God forgive me!'

She was five years nearer childhood than he, even taking into account the two years or more a girl child has advantage over the boys of her own age. She stood entranced, a little frightened by his intensity, and inexpressibly moved by the anguish she felt emanating from him like a raw, drowning odour. The long-fingered hand that held her shook terribly, his whole body quivered. She put up her own hand gently and closed it over his, uplifted out of her own wretchedness by his greater and more inexplicable distress.

'I dare not speak for God,' she said steadily, 'but whatever there may be for me to forgive, that I dare. It is not your fault that I love you. All you ever did was be kinder to me than ever man was since I left Wales. And I did know, love, you did tell me, if I had heeded then, you did tell me you were a man under vow. What it was you never told me, but never grieve, oh, my own soul, never grieve so . . .'

While they stood rapt, the sunset light had deepened, blazed and burned silently into

115

glowing ash, and the first feathery shade of twilight, like the passing of a swift's wings, fled across their faces and melted into sudden pearly, radiant light. Her wide eyes were brimming with tears, almost the match of his. When he stooped to her, there was no way of knowing which of them had begun the kiss.

*　　　*　　　*

The little bell for Compline sounded clearly through the gardens on so limpid an evening, and stirred Brother Cadfael out of his half-doze at once. He was accustomed, in this refuge of his maturity as surely as in the warfaring of his youth, to awake fresh and alert, as he fell asleep, making the most of the twin worlds of night and day. He rose and went out into the earliest glowing image of evening, and closed the door after him.

It was but a few moments back to church through the herbarium and the rose garden. He went briskly, happy with the beauty of the evening and the promise for the morrow, and never knew why he should look aside to westward in passing, unless it was that the whole expanse of the sky on that side was delicate, pure and warming, like a girl's blush. And there they were, two clear shadows clasped together in silhouette against the fire of the west, outlined on the crest above the slope to the invisible brook. Matthew and

Melangell, unmistakable, constrained still but in each other's arms, linked in a kiss that lasted while Brother Cadfael came, passed and slipped away to his different devotions, but with that image printed indelibly on his eyes, even in his prayers.

CHAPTER SEVEN

The outrider of the bishop-legate's envoy—or should he rather be considered the empress's envoy?—arrived within the town and was directed through to the gatehouse of the castle in mid-evening of that same twenty-first day of June, to be presented to Hugh Beringar just as he was marshalling a half-dozen men to go down to the bridge and take an unpredicted part in the plans of Master Simeon Poer and his associates. Who would almost certainly be armed, being so far from home and in hitherto unexplored territory. Hugh found the visitor an unwelcome hindrance, but was too well aware of the many perils hemming the king's party on every side to dismiss the herald without ceremony. Whatever this embassage might be, he needed to know it, and make due preparation to deal with it.

In the gatehouse guard-room he found himself facing a stolid middle-aged squire, who delivered his errand word perfect.

'My lord sheriff, the Lady of the English and the lord bishop of Winchester entreat you to receive in peace their envoy, who comes to you with offerings of peace and good order in their name, and in their name asks your aid in resolving the griefs of the kingdom. I come before to announce him.'

So the empress had assumed the traditional title of a queen-elect before her coronation! The matter began to look final.

'The lord bishop's envoy will be welcome,' said Hugh, 'and shall be received with all honour here in Shrewsbury. I will lend an attentive ear to whatever he may have to say to me. As at this moment I have an affair in hand which will not wait. How far ahead of your lord do you ride?'

'A matter of two hours, perhaps,' said the squire, considering.

'Good, then I can set forward all necessary preparations for his reception, and still have time to clear up a small thing I have in hand. With how many attendants does he come?'

'Two men-at-arms only, my lord, and myself.'

'Then I will leave you in the hands of my deputy, who will have lodgings made ready for you and your two men here in the castle. As for your lord, he shall come to my own house, and my wife shall make him welcome. Hold me excused if I make small ceremony now, for this business is a twilight matter, and will not

118

wait. Later I will see amends made.'

The messenger was well content to have his horse stabled and tended, and be led away by Alan Herbard to a comfortable lodging where he could shed his boots and leather coat, and be at his ease, and take his time and his pleasure over the meat and wine that was presently set before him. Hugh's young deputy would play the host very graciously. He was still new in office, and did everything committed to him with a flourish. Hugh left them to it, and took his half-dozen men briskly out through the town.

It was past Compline then, neither light nor dark, but hesitant between. By the time they reached the High Cross and turned down the steep curve of the Wyle they had their twilight eyes. In full darkness their quarry might have a better chance of eluding them, by daylight they would themselves have been too easily observed from afar. If these gamesters were experts they would have a lookout posted to give fair warning.

The Wyle, uncoiling eastward, brought them down to the town wall and the English gate, and there a thin, leggy child, shaggy-haired and bright-eyed, started out of the shadows under the gate to catch at Hugh's sleeve. Wat's boy, a sharp urchin of the Foregate, bursting with the importance of his errand and his own wit in managing it, had pinned down his quarry, and waited to inform and advise.

'My lord, they're met—all the four from the abbey, and a dozen or more from these parts, mostly from the town.' His note of scorn implied that they were sharper in the Foregate. 'You'd best leave the horses and go afoot. Riders out at this hour—they'd break and run as soon as you set hooves on the bridge. The sound carries.'

Good sense, that, if the meeting-place was close by. 'Where are they, then?' asked Hugh, dismounting.

'Under the far arch of the bridge, my lord—dry as a bone it is, and snug.' So it would be, with this low summer water. Only in full spate did the river prevent passage beneath that arch. In this fine season it would be a nest of dried-out grasses.

'They have a light, then?'

'A dark lantern. There's not a glimmer you'll see from either side unless you go down to the water, it sheds light only on the flat stone where they're throwing.'

Easily quenched, then, at the first alarm, and they would scatter like startled birds, every way. The fleecers would be the first and fleetest. The fleeced might well be netted in some numbers, but their offence was no more than being foolish at their own expense, not theft nor malpractice on any other.

'We leave the horses here,' said Hugh, making up his mind. 'You heard the boy. They're under the bridge, they'll have used the

120

path that goes down to the Gaye, along the riverside. The other side of the arch is thick bushes, but that's the way they'll break. Three men to either slope, and I'll bear with the western three. And let our own young fools by, if you can pick them out, but hold fast the strangers.'

In this fashion they went to their raiding. They crossed the bridge by ones and twos, above the Severn water green with weedy shallows and shimmering with reflected light, and took their places on either side, spaced among the fringing bushes of the bank. By the time they were in place the afterglow had dissolved and faded into the western horizon, and the night came down like a velvet hand. Hugh drew off to westward along the by-road until at length he caught the faint glimmer of light beneath the stone arch. They were there. If in such numbers, perhaps he should have held them in better respect and brought more men. But he did not want the townsmen. By all means let them sneak away to their beds and think better of their dreams of milking cows likely to prove drier than sand. It was the cheats he wanted. Let the provost of the town deal with his civic idiots.

He let the sky darken somewhat before he took them in. The summer night settled, soft wings folding, and no moon. Then, at his whistle, they moved down from either flank.

It was the close-set bushes on the bank,

rustling stealthily in a windless night, that betrayed their coming a moment too soon. Whoever was on watch, below there, had a sharp ear. There was a shrill whistle, suddenly muted. The lantern went out instantly, there was black dark under the solid stonework of the bridge. Down went Hugh and his men, abandoning stealth for speed. Bodies parted, collided, heaved and fled, with no sound but the panting and gasping of scared breath. Hugh's officers waded through bushes, closing down to seal the archway. Some of those thus penned beneath the bridge broke to left, some to right, not venturing to climb into waiting arms, but wading through the shallows and floundering even into deeper water. A few struck out for the opposite shore, local lads well acquainted with their river and its reaches, and water-borne, like its fish, almost from birth. Let them go, they were Shrewsbury born and bred. If they had lost money, more fools they, but let them get to their beds and repent in peace. If their wives would let them!

But there were those beneath the arch of the bridge who had not Severn water in their blood, and were less ready to wet more than their feet in even low water. And suddenly these had steel in their hands, and were weaving and slashing and stabbing their way through into the open as best they could, and without scruple. It did not last long. In the quaking dark, sprawled among the trampled grasses up the riverside, Hugh's six clung to such captives as they could grapple, and shook off trickles of blood from their own scratches and gashes. And diminishing in the darkness, the thresh and toss of bushes marked the flight of those who had got away. Unseen beneath the bridge, the deserted lantern and scattered dice, grave loss to a trickster who must now prepare a new set, lay waiting to be retrieved.

Hugh shook off a few drops of blood from a grazed arm, and went scrambling through the rough grass to the path leading up from the Gaye to the highroad and the bridge. Before him a shadowy body fled, cursing. Hugh launched a shout to reach the road ahead of them: 'Hold him! The law wants him!' Foregate and town might be on their way to bed, but there were always late strays, both lawful and unlawful, and some on both sides would joyfully take up such an invitation to mischief or justice, whichever way the mind happened to bend.

Above him, in the deep, soft summer night that now bore only a saffron thread along the west, an answering hail shrilled, startled and merry, and there were confused sounds of brief, breathless struggle. Hugh loped up to the highroad to see three shadowy horsemen halted at the approach to the bridge, two of them closed in to flank the first, and that first leaning slightly from his saddle to grip in one hand the collar of a panting figure that leaned against his mount heaving in breath, and with small energy to attempt anything besides.

'I think, sir,' said the captor, eyeing Hugh's approach, 'this may be what you wanted. It seemed to me that the law cried out for him? Am I then addressing the law in these parts?'

It was a fine, ringing voice, unaccustomed to subduing its tone. The soft dark did not disclose his face clearly, but showed a body erect in the saddle, supple, shapely, unquestionably young. He shifted his grip on the prisoner, as though to surrender him to a better claim. Thus all but released, the fugitive did not break free and run for it, but spread his feet and stood his ground, half-defiant, eyeing Hugh dubiously.

'I'm in your debt for a minnow, it seems,' said Hugh, grinning as he recognised the man he had been chasing. 'But I doubt I've let all the salmon get clear away up-river. We were about breaking up a parcel of cheating rogues come here looking for prey, but this young gentleman you have by the coat turns out to be merely one of the simpletons, our worthy goldsmith out of the town. Master Daniel, I doubt there's more gold and silver to be lost than gained, in the company you've been keeping.'

'It's no crime to make a match at dice,' muttered the young man, shuffling his feet sullenly in the dust of the road. 'My luck would have turned . . .'

'Not with the dice they brought with them. But true it's no crime to waste your evening and go home with empty pockets, and I've no charge to make against you, provided you go back now, and hand yourself over with the rest to my sergeant. Behave yourself prettily, and you'll be home by midnight.'

Master Daniel Aurifaber took his dismissal thankfully, and slouched back towards the bridge, to be gathered in among the captives. The sound of hooves crossing the bridge at a trot indicated that someone had run for the horses, and intended a hunt to westward, in the direction the birds of prey had taken. In less than a mile they would be safe in woodland, and it would take hounds to run them to earth. Small chance of hunting them down by night. On the morrow something might be attempted.

'This is hardly the welcome I intended for you,' said Hugh, peering up into the shadowy face above him. 'For you, I think, must be the envoy sent from the Empress Maud and the bishop of Winchester. Your herald arrived little more than an hour ago, I did not expect you quite so soon. I had thought I should be done with this matter by the time you came. My name is Hugh Beringar, I stand here as sheriff for King Stephen. Your men are provided for at the castle, I'll send a guide with them. You, sir, are my own guest, if you will do my house that honour.'

'You're very gracious,' said the empress's messenger blithely, 'and with all my heart I will. But had you not better first make up your accounts with these townsmen of yours, and let them creep away to their beds? My business can well wait a little longer.'

*   *   *

'Not the most successful action ever I planned,' Hugh owned later to Cadfael. 'I under-estimated both their hardihood and the amount of cold steel they'd have about them.'

There were four guests missing from Brother Denis's halls that night: Master Simeon Poer, merchant of Guildford; Walter Bagot, glover; John Shure, tailor; William Hales, farrier. Of these, William Hales lay that night in a stone cell in Shrewsbury castle, along with a travelling pedlar who had touted for them in the town, but the other three had all broken safely away, bar a few scratches and bruises, into the woods to westward, the most northerly outlying spinneys of the Long Forest, there to bed down in the warm night and count their injuries and their gains, which were considerable. They could not now return to the abbey or the town; the traffic would in any case have stood only one more night at a profit. Three nights are the most to be reckoned on, after that some aggrieved wretch is sure to grow suspicious. Nor could they yet

126

venture south again. But the man who lives on his wits must keep them well honed and adaptable, and there are more ways than one of making a dishonest living.

As for the young rufflers and simple tradesmen who had come out with visions of rattling their winnings on the way home to their wives, they were herded into the gatehouse to be chided, warned, and sent home chapfallen, with very little in their pockets.

And there the night's work would have ended, if the flare of the torch under the gateway had not caught the metal gleam of a ring on Daniel Aurifaber's right hand, flat silver with an oval bezel, for one instant sharply defined. Hugh saw it, and laid a hand on the goldsmith's arm to detain him.

'That ring—let me see it closer!'

Daniel handed it over with a hint of reluctance, though it seemed to stem rather from bewilderment than from any feeling of guilt. It fitted closely, and passed over his knuckle with slight difficulty, but the finger bore no sign of having worn it regularly.

'Where did you get this?' asked Hugh, holding it under the flickering light to examine the device and inscription.

'I bought it honestly,' said Daniel defensively.

'That I need not doubt. But from whom? From one of those gamesters? Which one?'

'The merchant—Simeon Poer he called himself. He offered it, and it was a good piece of work. I paid well for it.'

'You have paid double for it, my friend,' said Hugh, 'for you bid fair to lose ring and money and all. Did it never enter your mind that it might be stolen?'

By the single nervous flutter of the goldsmith's eyelids the thought had certainly occurred to him, however hurriedly he had put it out of his mind again. 'No! Why should I think so? He seemed a stout, prosperous person, all he claimed to be . . .'

'This very morning,' said Hugh, 'just such a ring was taken during Mass from a pilgrim at the abbey. Abbot Radulfus sent word up to the provost, after they had searched thoroughly within the pale, in case it should be offered for sale in the market. I had the description of it in turn from the provost. This is the device and inscription of the bishop of Winchester, and it was given to the bearer to secure him safe-conduct on the road.'

'But I bought it in good faith,' protested Daniel, dismayed. 'I paid the man what he asked, the ring is mine, honestly come by.'

'From a thief. Your misfortune, lad, and it may teach you to be more wary of sudden kind acquaintances in the future who offer you rings to buy—wasn't it so?—at somewhat less than you know to be their value? Travelling men rattling dice give nothing for nothing, but take whatever they can get. If they've emptied your purse for you, take warning for the next time. This must go back to the lord abbot in the morning. Let him deal with the owner.' He saw the goldsmith draw angry breath to complain of his deprivation, and shook his head to ward off the effort, not unkindly. 'You have no remedy. Bite your tongue, Daniel, and go make your peace with your wife.'

*   *   *

The empress's envoy rode gently up the Wyle in the deepening dark, keeping pace with Hugh's smaller mount. His own was a fine, tall beast, and the young man in the saddle was long of body and limb. Afoot, thought Hugh, studying him sidelong, he will top me by a head. Very much of an age with me, I might give him a year or two, hardly more.

'Were you ever in Shrewsbury before?'

'Never. Once, perhaps, I was just within the shire, I am not sure how the border runs. I was near Ludlow once. This abbey of yours, I marked it as I came by, a very fine, large enclosure. They keep the Benedictine Rule?'

'They do.' Hugh expected further questions, but they did not come. 'You have kinsmen in the Order?'

Even in the dark he was aware of his companion's grave, musing smile. 'In a manner of speaking, yes, I have. I think he would give

129

me leave to call him so, though there is no blood-kinship. One who used me like a son. I keep a kindness for the habit, for his sake. And did I hear you say there are pilgrims here now? For some particular feast?'

'For the translation of Saint Winifred, who was brought here four years ago from Wales. Tomorrow is the day of her arrival.' Hugh had spoken by custom, quite forgetting what Cadfael had told him of that arrival, but the mention of it brought his friend's story back sharply to mind. 'I was not in Shrewsbury then,' he said, withholding judgement. 'I brought my manors to King Stephen's support the following year. My own country is the north of the shire.'

They had reached the top of the hill, and were turning towards Saint Mary's church. The great gate of Hugh's courtyard stood wide, with torches at the gateposts, waiting for them. His message had been faithfully delivered to Aline, and she was waiting for them with all due ceremony, the bedchamber prepared, the meal ready to come to table. All rules, all times, bow to the coming of a guest, the duty and privilege of hospitality.

She met them at the door, opening it wide to welcome them in. They stepped into the hall, and into a flood of light from torches at the walls and candles on the table, and instinctively they turned to face each other, taking the first long look. It grew ever longer as their intent eyes grew wider. It was a question which of them groped towards recognition first. Memory pricked and realisation awoke almost stealthily. Aline stood smiling and wondering, but mute, eyeing first one, then the other, until they should stir and shed a clearer light.

'But I know you!' said Hugh. 'Now I see you, I do know you.'

'I have seen you before,' agreed the guest. 'I was never in this shire but the once, and yet...'

'It needed light to see you by,' said Hugh, 'for I never heard your voice but the once, and then no more than a few words. I doubt if you even remember them, but I do. Six words only. "Now have ado with a man!" you said. And your name, your name I never heard but in a manner I take as it was meant. You are Robert, the forester's son who fetched Yves Hugonin out of that robber fortress up on Titterstone Clee. And took him home with you, I think, and his sister with him.'

'And you are that officer who laid the siege that gave me the cover I needed,' cried the guest, gleaming. 'Forgive me that I hid from you then, but I had no warranty there in your territory. How glad I am to meet you honestly now, with no need to take to flight.'

'And no need now to be Robert, the forester's son,' said Hugh, elated and smiling. 'My name I have given you, and the freedom

131

of this house I offer with it. Now may I know yours?'

'In Antioch, where I was born,' said the guest, 'I was called Daoud. But my father was an Englishman of Robert of Normandy's force, and among his comrades in arms I was baptised a Christian, and took the name of the priest who stood my godfather. Now I bear the name of Olivier de Bretagne.'

*   *   *

They sat late into the night together, savouring each other now face to face, after a year and a half of remembering and wondering. But first, as was due, they made short work of Olivier's errand here.

'I am sent,' he said seriously, 'to urge all sheriffs of shires to consider, whatever their previous fealty, whether they should not now accept the proffered peace under the Empress Maud, and take the oath of loyalty to her. This is the message of the bishop and the council: This land has all too long been torn between two factions, and suffered great damage and loss through their mutual enmity. And here *I* say that I lay no blame on that party which is not my own, for there are valid claims on both sides, and equally the blame falls on both for failing to come to some agreement to end these distresses. The fortune at Lincoln might just as well have fallen the opposing way, but it fell as it did, and England is left with a king made captive, and a queen-elect free and in the ascendant. Is it not time to call a halt? For the sake of order and peace and the sound regulation of the realm, and to have a government in command which can and must put down the many injustices and tyrannies which you know, as well as I, have set themselves up outside all law. Surely any strong rule is better than no rule at all. For the sake of peace and order, will you not accept the empress, and hold your county in allegiance to her? She is already in Westminster now, the preparations for her coronation go forward. There is a far better prospect of success if all sheriffs come in to strengthen her rule.'

'You are asking me,' said Hugh gently, 'to go back on my sworn fealty to King Stephen.'

'Yes,' agreed Olivier honestly, 'I am. For weighty reasons, and in no treasonous mind. You need not love, only forbear from hating. Think of it rather as keeping your fealty to the people of this county of yours, and this land.'

'That I can do as well or better on the side where I began,' said Hugh, smiling. 'It is what I am doing now, as best I can. It is what I will continue to do while I have breath. I am King Stephen's man, and I will not desert him.'

'Ah, well!' said Olivier, smiling and sighing in the same breath. 'To tell you truth, now I've met you, I expected nothing less. I would not go from my oath, either. My lord is the empress's man, and I am my lord's man, and if our positions were changed round, my answer would be the same as yours. Yet there is truth in what I have pleaded. How much can a people bear? Your labourer in the fields, your little townsman with a bare living to be looted from him, these would be glad to settle for Stephen or for Maud, only to be rid of the other. And I do what I am sent out to do, as well as I can.'

'I have no fault to find with the matter or the manner,' said Hugh. 'Where next do you go? Though I hope you will not go for a day or two, I would know you better, and we have a great deal to talk over, you and I.'

'From here north-east to Stafford, Derby, Nottingham, and back by the eastern parts. Some will come to terms, as some lords have done already. Some will hold to their own king, like you. And some will do as they have done before, go back and forth like a weather-cock with the wind, and put up their price at every change. No matter, we have done with that now.'

He leaned forward over the table, setting his wine-cup aside. 'I had—I have—another errand of my own, and I should be glad to stay with you a few days, until I have found what I'm seeking, or made certain it is not here to be found. Your mention of this flood of pilgrims for the feast gives me a morsel of hope. A man who wills to be lost could find cover among so many, all strangers to one another. I am looking for a young man called Luc Meverel. He has not, to your knowledge, made his way here?'

'Not by that name,' said Hugh, interested and curious. 'But a man who willed to be lost might choose to doff his own name. What's your need of him?'

'Not mine. It's a lady who wants him back. You may not have got word, this far north,' said Olivier, 'of everything that happened in Winchester during the council. There was a death there that came all too near to me. Did you hear of it? King Stephen's queen sent her clerk there with a bold challenge to the legate's authority, and the man was attacked for his audacity in the street by night, and got off with his life only at the cost of another life.'

'We have indeed heard of it,' said Hugh with kindling interest. 'Abbot Radulfus was there at the council, and brought back a full report. A knight by the name of Rainald Bossard, who came to the clerk's aid when he was set upon. One of those in the service of Laurence d'Angers, so we heard.'

'Who is my lord, also.'

'By your good service to his kin at Bromfield that was plain enough. I thought of you when the abbot spoke of d'Angers, though I had no name for you then. Then this man Bossard was well known to you?'

'Through a year of service in Palestine, and the voyage home together. A good man he was, and a good friend to me, and struck down in defending his honest opponent. I was not with him that night, I wish I had been, he might yet be alive. But he had only one or two of his own people, not in arms. There were five or six set on the clerk, it was a wretched business, confused and in the dark. The murderer got clean away, and has never been traced. Rainald's wife ... Juliana ... I did not know her until we came with our lord to Winchester, Rainald's chief manor is nearby. I have learned,' said Olivier very gravely, 'to hold her in the highest regard. She was her lord's true match, and no one could say more or better of any lady.'

'There is an heir?' asked Hugh. 'A man grown, or still a child?'

'No, they never had children. Rainald was nearly fifty, she cannot be many years younger. And very beautiful,' said Olivier with solemn consideration, as one attempting not to praise, but to explain. 'Now she's widowed she'll have a hard fight on her hands to evade being married off again—for she'll want no other after Rainald. She has manors of her own to bestow. They had thought of the inheritance, the two of them together, that's why they took into their household this young man Luc Meverel, only a year ago. He is a distant cousin of Dame Juliana, twenty-four or

136

twenty-five years old, I suppose, and landless. They meant to make him their heir.'

He fell silent for some minutes, frowning past the guttering candles, his chin in his palm. Hugh studied him, and waited. It was a face worth studying, clean-boned, olive-skinned, fiercely beautiful, even with the golden, falcon's eyes thus hooded. The blue-black hair that clustered thickly about his head, clasping like folded wings, shot sullen bluish lights back from the candle's waverings. Daoud, born in Antioch, son of an English crusading soldier in Robert of Normandy's following, somehow blown across the world in the service of an Angevin baron, to fetch up here almost more Norman than the Normans ... The world, thought Hugh, is not so great, after all, but a man born to venture may bestride it.

'I have been three times in that household,' said Olivier, 'but I never knowingly set eyes on this Luc Meverel. All I know of him is what others have said, but among the others I take my choice which voice to believe. There is no one, man or woman, in that manor but agrees he was utterly devoted to Dame Juliana. But as to the manner of his devotion ... There are many who say he loved her far too well, by no means after the fashion of a son. Again, some say he was equally loyal to Rainald, but their voices are growing fainter now. Luc was one of those with his lord when Rainald was stabbed to death in the street. And two days later he

137

vanished from his place, and has not been seen since.'

'Now I begin to see,' said Hugh, drawing in cautious breath. 'Have they gone so far as to say this man slew his lord in order to gain his lady?'

'It is being said now, since his flight. Who began the whisper there's no telling, but by this time it's grown into a bellow.'

'Then why should he run from the prize for which he had played? It makes poor sense. If he had stayed there need have been no such whispers.'

'Ah, but I think there would have been, whether he went or stayed. There were those who grudged him his fortune, and would have welcomed any means of damaging him. They are finding two good reasons, now, why he should break and run. The first, pure guilt and remorse, too late to save any one of the three of them. The second, fear—fear that someone had got wind of his act, and meant to fetch out the truth at all costs. Either way, a man might break and take to his heels. What you kill for may seem even less attainable,' said Olivier with rueful shrewdness, 'once you have killed.'

'But you have not yet told me,' said Hugh, 'what the lady says of him. Hers is surely a voice that should be heeded.'

'She says that such a vile suspicion is impossible. She did, she does, value her young cousin, but not in the way of love, nor will she have it that he has ever entertained such thoughts of her. She says he would have died for his lord, and that it is his lord's death which has driven him away, sick with grief, a little mad—who knows how deluded and haunted? For he was there that night, he saw Rainald die. She is sure of him. She wants him found and brought back to her. She looks upon him as a son, and now more than ever she needs him.'

'And it's for her sake you're seeking him. But why look for him here, northwards? He may have gone south, west, across the sea by the Kentish ports. Why to the north?'

'Because we have just one word of him since he was lost from his place, and that was going north on the road to Newbury. I came by that same way, by Abingdon and Oxford, and I have enquired for him everywhere, a young man travelling alone. But I can only seek him by his own name, for I know no other for him. As you say, who knows what he may be calling himself now!'

'And you don't even know what he looks like—nothing but merely his age? You're hunting for a spectre!'

'What is lost can always be found, it needs only enough patience.' Olivier's hawk's face, beaked and passionate, did not suggest patience, but the set of his lips was stubborn and pure in absolute resolution.

'Well, at least,' said Hugh, considering, 'we

may go down to see Saint Winifred brought home to her altar, tomorrow, and Brother Denis can run through the roster of his pilgrims for us, and point out any who are of the right age and kind, solitary or not. As for strangers here in the town, I fancy Provost Corviser should be able to put his finger on most of them. Every man knows every man in Shrewsbury. But the abbey is the more likely refuge, if he's here at all.' He pondered, gnawing a thoughtful lip. 'I must send the ring down to the abbot at first light, and let him know what's happened to his truant guests, but before I may go down to the feast myself I must send out a dozen men and have them beat the near reaches of the woods to westward for our game birds. If they're over the border, so much the worse for Wales, and I can do no more, but I doubt if they intend to live wild any longer than they need. They may not go far. How if I should leave you with the provost, to pick his brains for your quarry here within the town, while I go hunting for mine? Then we'll go down together to see the brothers bring their saint home, and talk to Brother Denis concerning the list of his guests.'

'That would suit me well,' said Olivier gladly. 'I should like to pay my respects to the lord abbot, I do recall seeing him in Winchester, though he would not notice me. And there was a brother of that house, if you recall,' he said, his golden eyes veiled within long black lashes that swept his fine cheekbones, 'who was with you at Bromfield and up on Clee, that time . . . You must know him well. He is still here at the abbey?'

'He is. He'll be back in his bed now after Lauds. And you and I had better be thinking of seeking ours, if we're to be busy tomorrow.'

'He was good to my lord's young kinsfolk,' said Olivier. 'I should like to see him again.'

No need to ask for a name, thought Hugh, eyeing him with a musing smile. And indeed, should he know the name? He had not mentioned any, when he spoke of one who was no blood-kin, but who had used him like a son, one for whose sake he kept a kindness for the Benedictine habit.

'You shall!' said Hugh, and rose in high content to marshal his guest to the bedchamber prepared for him.

CHAPTER EIGHT

Abbot Radulfus was up long before Prime on the festal morning, and so were his obedientiaries, all of whom had their important tasks in preparation for the procession. When Hugh's messenger presented himself at the abbot's lodging the dawn was still fresh, dewy and cool, the light lying brightly across the roofs while the great court lay in lilac-tinted shadow. In the gardens every tree and bush cast a long band of shade, striping the flower-beds like giant brush-strokes in some gilded illumination.

The abbot received the ring with astonished pleasure, relieved of one flaw that might have marred the splendour of the day. 'And you say these malefactors were guests in our halls, all four? We are well rid of them, but if they are armed, as you say, and have taken to the woods close by, we shall need to warn our travellers, when they leave us.'

'My lord Beringar has a company out beating the edges of the forest for them this moment,' said the messenger. 'There was nothing to gain by following them in the dark, once they were in cover. But by daylight we'll hope to trace them. One we have safe in hold, he may tell us more about them, where they're from, and what they have to answer for elsewhere. But at least now they can't hinder your festivities.'

'And for that I'm devoutly thankful. As this man Ciaran will certainly be for the recovery of his ring.' He added, with a glance aside at the breviary that lay on his desk, and a small frown for the load of ceremonial that lay before him for the next few hours: 'Shall we not see the lord sheriff here for Mass this morning?'

'Yes, Father, he does intend it, and he brings

142

a guest also. He had first to set this hunt in motion, but before Mass they will be here.'

'He has a guest?'

'An envoy from the empress's court came last night, Father. A man of Laurence d'Angers' household, Olivier de Bretagne.'

The name that had meant nothing to Hugh meant as little to Radulfus, though he nodded recollection and understanding at mention of the young man's overlord. 'Then will you say to Hugh Beringar that I beg he and his guest will remain after Mass, and dine with me here. I should be glad to make the acquaintance of Messire de Bretagne, and hear his news.'

'I will so tell him, Father,' said the messenger, and forthwith took his leave.

Left alone in his parlour, Abbot Radulfus stood for a moment looking down thoughtfully at the ring in his palm. The sheltering hand of the bishop-legate would certainly be a powerful protection to any traveller so signally favoured, wherever there existed any order or respect for law, whether in England or Wales. Only those already outside the pale of law, with lives or liberty already forfeit if taken, would defy so strong a sanction. After this crowning day many of the guests here would be leaving again for home. He must not forget to give due warning, before they dispersed, that malefactors might be lurking at large in the woods to westward, and that they were armed, and all too handy at using their daggers. Best that the pilgrims should make sure of leaving in companies stout enough to discourage assault.

Meantime, there was satisfaction in returning to one pilgrim, at least, his particular armour.

The abbot rang the little bell that lay upon his desk, and in a few moments Brother Vitalis came to answer the summons.

'Will you enquire at the guest-hall, brother, for the man called Ciaran, and bid him here to speak with me?'

* * *

Brother Cadfael had also risen well before Prime, and gone to open his workshop and kindle his brazier into cautious and restrained life, in case it should be needed later to prepare tisanes for some ecstatic souls carried away by emotional excitement, or warm applications for weaker vessels trampled in the crowd. He was used to the transports of simple souls caught up in far from simple raptures.

He had a few things to tend to, and was happy to deal with them alone. Young Oswin was entitled to his fill of sleep until the bell awoke him. Very soon now he would graduate to the hospital of Saint Giles, where the reliquary of Saint Winifred now lay, and the unfortunates who carried their contagion with them, and might not be admitted into the town, could find rest, care and shelter for as long as they needed it. Brother Mark, that dearly-missed disciple, was gone from there now, already ordained deacon, his eyes fixed ahead upon his steady goal of priesthood. If ever he cast a glance over his shoulder, he would find nothing but encouragement and affection, the proper harvest of the seed he had sown. Oswin might not be such another, but he was a good enough lad, and would do honestly by the unfortunates who drifted into his care.

Cadfael went down to the banks of the Meole brook, the westward boundary of the enclave, where the pease-fields declined to the sunken summer water. The rays from the east were just being launched like lances over the high roofs of the monastic buildings, and piercing the scattered copses beyond the brook, and the grassy banks on the further side. This same water, drawn off much higher in its course, supplied the monastery fish-ponds, the hatchery, and the mill and millpond beyond, and was fed back into the brook just before it entered the Severn. It lay low enough now, an archipelago of shoals, half sand, half grass and weed, spreading smooth islands across its breadth. After this spell, thought Cadfael, we shall need plenty of rain. But let that wait a day or two.

He turned back to climb the slope again. The earlier field of pease had already been gleaned, the second would be about ready for harvesting after the festival. A couple of days, and all the excitement would be over, and the horarium of the house and the cycle of the seasons would resume their imperturbable progress, two enduring rhythms in the desperately variable fortunes of mankind. He turned along the path to his workshop, and there was Melangell hesitating before its closed door.

She heard his step in the gravel behind her, and looked round with a bright, expectant face. The pearly morning light became her, softened the coarseness of her linen gown, and smoothed cool lilac shadows round the childlike curves of her face. She had gone to great pains to prepare herself fittingly for the day's solemnities. Her skirts were spotless, crisped out with care, her dark-gold hair, burning with coppery lustre, braided and coiled on her head in a bright crown, its tight plaits drawing up the skin of her temples and cheeks so strongly that her brows were pulled aslant, and the dark-lashed blue eyes elongated and made mysterious. But the radiance that shone from her came not from the sun's caresses, but from within. The blue of those eyes burned as brilliantly as the blue of the gentians Cadfael had seen long ago in the mountains of southern France, on his way to the east. The ivory and rose of her cheeks glowed. Melangell was in the highest state of hope, happiness and expectation.

She made him a very pretty reverence, flushing and smiling, and held out to him the little vial of poppy-syrup he had given to Rhun three days ago. Still unopened!

'If you please, Brother Cadfael, I have brought this back to you. And Rhun prays that it may serve some other who needs it more, and with the more force because he has endured without it.'

He took it from her gently and held it in his cupped hand, a crude little vial stopped with a wooden stopper and a membrane of very thin parchment tied with a waxed thread to seal it. All intact. The boy's third night here, and he had submitted to handling and been mild and biddable in all, but when the means of oblivion was put into his hand and left to his private use, he had preserved it, and with it some core of his own secret integrity, at his own chosen cost. God forbid, thought Cadfael, that I should meddle there. Nothing short of a saint should knock on that door.

'You are not angry with him?' asked Melangell anxiously, but smiling still, unable to believe that any shadow should touch the day, now that her love had clasped and kissed her. 'Because he did not drink it? It was not that he ever doubted *you*. He said so to me. He said— I never quite understand him!—he said it was a time for offering, and he had his offering prepared.'

Cadfael asked: 'Did he sleep?' To have deliverance in hand, even unopened, might well bring peace. 'Hush, now, no, how could I be angry! But *did* he sleep?'

'He says that he did. I think it must be true, he looks so fresh and young. I prayed hard for him.' With all the force of her new happiness, loaded with bliss she felt the need to pour out upon all those near to her. In the conveyance of blessedness by affection Cadfael firmly believed.

'You prayed well,' said Cadfael. 'Never doubt he has gained by it. I'll keep this for some soul in worse need, as Rhun says. It will have the virtue of his faith to strengthen it. I shall see you both during the day.'

She went away from him with a light, springing step and a head reared to breathe in the very space and light of the sky. And Cadfael went in to make sure he had everything ready to provide for a long and exhausting day.

So Rhun had arrived at the last frontier of belief, and fallen, or emerged, or soared into the region where the soul realises that pain is of no account, that to be within the secret of God is more than well being, and past the power of the tongue to utter. To embrace the decree of pain is to translate it, to shed it like a rain of blessing on others who have not yet understood.

Who am I, thought Cadfael, alone in the

148

solitude of his workshop, that I should dare to ask for a sign? If he can endure and ask nothing, must not I be ashamed of doubting?

*   *   *

Melangell passed with a dancing step along the path from the herbarium. On her right hand the western sky soared, in such reflected if muted brightness that she could not forbear from turning to stare into it. A counter-tide of light flowed in here from the west, surging up the slope from the brook and spilling over the crest into the garden. Somewhere on the far side of the entire monastic enclave the two tides would meet, and the light of the west falter, pale and die before the onslaught from the east; but here the bulk of guest-hall and church cut off the newly-risen sun, and left the field to this hesitant and soft-treading antidawn.

There was someone labouring along the far border of the flower-garden, going delicately on still tender feet, watching where he trod. He was alone. No attendant shadow appeared at his back, yesterday's magic still held. She was staring at Ciaran, Ciaran without Matthew. That in itself was a minor miracle, to bring in this day made for miracles.

Melangell watched him begin to descend the slope towards the brook, and when he was no more than a head and shoulders black against the brightness, she suddenly turned and went after him. The path down to the water skirted the growing pease, keeping close to a hedge of thick bushes above the mill-pool. Halfway down the slope she halted, uncertain whether to intrude on his solitude. Ciaran had reached the waterside, and stood surveying what looked like a safe green floor, dappled here and there with the bleached islands of sand, and studded with a few embedded rocks that stood dry from three weeks of fine weather. He looked upstream and down, even stepped into the shallow water that barely covered his naked feet, and surely soothed and refreshed them. Yet how strange, that he should be here alone! Never, until yesterday, had she seen either of these two without the other, yet now they went apart.

She was on the point of stealing away to leave him undisturbed when she saw what he was doing. He had some tiny thing in his hand, into which he was threading a thin cord, and knotting the cord to hold it fast. When he raised both hands to make fast the end of his cord to the tether that held the cross about his neck, the small talisman swung free into the light and glimmered for an instant in silver, before he tucked it away within the neck of his shirt, out of sight against his breast. Then she knew what it was, and stirred in pure pleasure for him, and uttered a small, breathless sound. For Ciaran had his ring again, the safe-conduct that was to ensure him passage to his journey's end.

He had heard her, and swung about, startled and wary. She stood shaken and disconcerted, and then, knowing herself discovered, ran down the last slope of grass to his side. 'They've found it for you!' she said breathlessly, in haste to fill the silence between them and dispel her own uneasiness at having seemed to spy upon him. 'Oh, I am glad! Is the thief taken, then?'

'Melangell!' he said. 'You're early abroad, too? Yes, you see I am blessed, after all, I have it again. The lord abbot restored it to me only some minutes ago. But no, the thief is not caught, he and some fellow-rogues are fled into the woods, it seems. But I can go forth again without fear now.'

His dark eyes, deep-set under thick brows, opened wide upon her, smiling, holding her charmed in the abrupt discovery that he was, despite his disease, a young and comely man, who should have been in the fulness of his powers. Either she was imagining it, or he stood a little straighter, a little taller, than she had ever yet seen him, and the burning intensity of his face had mellowed into a brighter, more human ardour, as if some foreglow of the day's spiritual radiance had given him new hope.

'Melangell,' he said in a soft, vehement rush of words, 'you can't guess how glad I am of this

151

meeting, it was God sent you here to me. I've long wanted to speak to you alone. Never think that because I myself am doomed, I can't see what's before my eyes concerning others who are dear to me. I have something to ask of you, to beg of you, most earnestly. Don't tell Matthew that I have my ring again!'

'Does he not know?' she asked, astray.

'No, he was not by when the abbot sent for me. He must not know! Keep my secret, if you love him—if you have some pity, at least for me. I have told no one, and you must not. The lord abbot is not likely to speak of it to any other, why should he? That he would leave to me. If you and I keep silent, there's no need for anyone else to find out.'

Melangell was lost. She saw him through a rainbow of starting tears, for very pity of his long face hollowed in shade, his eyes glowing like the quiet, living heart of a banked fire.

'But why? Why do you want to keep it from him?'

'For his sake and yours—yes, and mine! Do you think I have not understood long ago that he loves you?—that you feel as much also for him? Only I stand in the way! It's bitter to know it, and I would have it changed. My one wish now is that you and he should be happy together. If he loves me so faithfully, may not I also love him? You know him! He will sacrifice himself, and you, and all things beside, to finish what he has undertaken, and see me safe into Aberdaron. I don't accept his sacrifice, I won't endure it! Why should you both be wretched, when my one wish is to go to my rest in peace of mind and leave my friend happy? Now, while he feels secure that I dare not set out without the ring, for God's sake, girl, leave him in innocence. *And I will go*, and leave you both my blessing.'

Melangell stood quivering, like a leaf shaken by the soft, vehement wind of his words, uncertain even of her own heart. 'Then what must I do? What is it you want of me?'

'Keep my secret,' said Ciaran, 'and go with Matthew in this holy procession. Oh, he'll go with you, and be glad. He won't wonder that I should stay behind and wait the saint's coming here within the pale. And while you're gone, I'll go on my way. My feet are almost healed, I have my ring again, I shall reach my haven. You need not be afraid for me. Only keep him happy as long as you may, and even when my going is known, then use your arts, keep him, hold him fast. That's all I shall ever ask of you.'

'But he'll know,' she said, alert to dangers. 'The porter will tell him you're gone, as soon as he looks for you and asks.'

'No, for I shall go by this way, across the brook and out to the west, for Wales. The porter will not see me go. See, it's barely ankle-deep in this season. I have kinsmen in Wales, the first miles are nothing. And among so great a throng, if he does look for me, he'll hardly wonder at not finding me. Not for hours need he so much as think of me, if you do your part. You take care of Matthew, I will absolve both you and him of all care of me, for I shall do well enough. All the better for knowing I leave him safe with you. For you do love him,' said Ciaran softly.

'Yes,' said Melangell in a long sigh.

'Then take and hold him, and my blessing on you both. You may tell him—but well afterwards!—that it is what I designed and intended,' he said, and suddenly and briefly smiled at some unspoken thought he did not wish to share with her.

'You will really do this for him and for me? You mean it? You would go on alone for his sake ... Oh, you are good!' she said passionately, and caught at his hand and pressed it to her heart for an instant, for he was giving her the whole world at his own sorrowful cost, and for selfless love of his friend, and there might never be any time but this one moment even to thank him. 'I'll never forget your goodness. All my life long I shall pray for you.'

'No,' said Ciaran, the same dark smile plucking at his lips as she released his hand, 'forget me, and help him to forget me. That is the best gift you can make me. And better you should not speak to me again. Go and find him. That's your part, and I depend on you.'

She drew back from him a few paces, her

eyes still fixed on him in gratitude and worship, made him a strange little reverence with head and hands, and turned obediently to climb the field into the garden. By the time she reached level ground and began to thread the beds of the rose garden she was breaking into a joyous run.

*   *   *

They gathered in the great court as soon as everyone, monk, lay servant, guest and townsman, had broken his fast. Seldom had the court seen such a crowd, and outside the walls the Foregate was loud with voices, as the guildsmen of Shrewsbury, provost, elders and all, assembled to join the solemn procession that would set out for Saint Giles. Half of the choir monks, led by Prior Robert, were to go in procession to fetch home the reliquary, while the abbot and the remaining brothers waited to greet them with music and candles and flowers on their return. As for the devout of town and Foregate, and the pilgrims within the walls, they might form and follow Prior Robert, such of them as were able-bodied and eager, while the lame and feeble might wait with the abbot, and prove their devotion by labouring out at least a little way to welcome the saint on her return.

'I should so much like to go with them all the way,' said Melangell, flushed and excited among the chattering, elbowing crowd in the court. 'It is not far. But too far for Rhun—he could not keep pace.'

He was there beside her, very silent, very white, very fair, as though even his flaxen hair had turned paler at the immensity of this experience. He leaned on his crutches between his sister and Dame Alice, and his crystal eyes were very wide, and looked very far, as though he was not even aware of their solicitude hemming him in on either side. Yet he answered simply enough, 'I should like to go a little way, at least, until they leave me behind. But you need not wait for me.'

'As though I would leave you!' said Mistress Weaver, comfortably clucking. 'You and I will keep together and see the pilgrimage out to the best we can, and heaven will be content with that. But the girl has her legs, she may go all the way, and put up a few prayers for you going and returning, and we'll none of us be the worse for it.'

She leaned to twitch the neck of his shirt and the collar of his coat into immaculate neatness, and to fuss over his extreme pallor, afraid he was coming down with illness from over-excitement, though he seemed tranquil as ivory, and serenely absent in spirit, gone somewhere she could not follow. Her hand, rough-fingered from weaving, smoothed his well-brushed hair, teasing every tendril back from his tall forehead.

156

'Run off, then, child,' she said to Melangell, without turning from the boy. 'But find someone we know. There'll be riffraff running alongside, I dare say—no escaping them. Stay by Mistress Glover, or the apothecary's widow ...'

'Matthew is going with them,' said Melangell, flushing and smiling at his very name. 'He told me so. I met him when we came from Prime.'

It was only half-true. She had rather confided boldly to him that she wished to tread every step of the way, and at every step remember and intercede for the souls she most loved on earth. No need to name them. He, no doubt, thought with reflected tenderness of her brother; but she was thinking no less of this anguished pair whose fortunes she now carried delicately and fearfully in her hands. She had even said, greatly venturing, 'Ciaran cannot keep pace, poor soul, he must wait here, like Rhun. But can't we make our steps count for them?'

But for all that, Matthew had looked over his shoulder, and hesitated a sharp instant before he turned his face fully to her, and said abruptly: 'Yes, we'll go, you and I. Yes, let's go that short way together, surely I have the right, this once ... I'll make my prayers for Rhun every step of the way.'

'Trot and find him, then, girl,' said Dame Alice, satisfied. 'Matthew will take good care

157

of you. See, they're forming up, you'd best hurry. We'll be here to watch you come in.'

Melangell fled, elated. Prior Robert had drawn up his choir, with Brother Anselm the precentor at their head, facing the gate. The shifting, murmuring, excited column of pilgrims formed up at his rear, twitching like a dragon's tail, a long, brightly-coloured, volatile train, brave with flowers, lighted tapers, offerings, crosses and banners. Matthew was waiting to reach out an eager hand to her and draw her in beside him. 'You have leave? She trusts you to me . . . ?'

'You're not troubled about Ciaran?' she could not forbear asking anxiously. 'He's right to stay here, he couldn't manage the walk.'

The choir monks before them began their processional psalm, Prior Robert led the way through the open gate, and after him went the brothers in their ordered pairs, and after them the notabilities of the town, and after them the long retinue of pilgrims, crowding forward eagerly, picking up the chant where they had knowledge of it or a sensitive ear, pouring out past the gatehouse and turning right towards Saint Giles.

*   *   *

Brother Cadfael went with Prior Robert's party, with Brother Adam of Reading walking beside him. Along the broad road by the enclave wall, past the great triangle of trodden grass at the horse-fair ground, and again bearing right with the road, between scattered houses and sun-bleached pastures and fields to the very edge of the suburb, where the squat tower of the hospital church, the roof of the hospice, and the long wattle fence of its garden showed dark against the bright eastern sky, slightly raised from the road on a gentle green mound. And all the way the long train of followers grew longer and more gaily-coloured, as the people of the Foregate in their best holiday clothes came out from their dwellings and joined the procession.

There was no room in the small, dark church for more than the brothers and the civic dignitaries of the town. The rest gathered all about the doorway, craning to get a glimpse of the proceedings within. With his lips moving almost soundlessly on the psalms and prayers, Cadfael watched the play of candle-light on the silver tracery that ornamented Saint Winifred's elegant oak coffin, elevated there on the altar as when they had first brought it from Gwytherin, four years earlier. He wondered whether his motive in securing for himself a place among the eight brothers who would bear her back to the abbey had been as pure as he had hoped. Had he been staking a proprietory claim on her, as one who had been at her first coming? Or had he meant it as a humble and penitential gesture? He was, after all, past sixty, and as he recalled, the oak casket was heavy, its edges sharp on a creaky shoulder, and the way back long enough to bring out all the potential discomforts. She might yet find a way of showing him whether she approved his proceedings or no, by striking him helpless with rheumatic pains!

The office ended. The eight chosen brothers, matched in height and pace, lifted the reliquary and settled it upon their shoulders. The prior stooped his lofty head through the low doorway into the mid-morning radiance, and the crowd clustered about the church opened to make way for the saint to ride to her triumph. The procession reformed, Prior Robert before with the brothers, the coffin with its bearers, flanked by crosses and banners and candles, and eager women bringing garlands of flowers. With measured pace, with music and solemn joy, Saint Winifred—or whatever represented her there in the sealed and secret place—was borne back to her own altar in the abbey church.

Curious, thought Cadfael, carefully keeping the step by numbers, it seems lighter than I remember. Is that possible? In only four years? He was familiar with the curious propensities of the body, dead or alive, he had once been led into a gallery of caverns in the desert where ancient Christians had lived and died, he knew what dry air can do to flesh,

160

preserving the light and shrivelled shell while the juice of life was drawn off into spirit. Whatever was there in the reliquary, it rode tranquilly upon his shoulder, like a light hand guiding him. It was not heavy at all!

CHAPTER NINE

Something wonderful happened along the way to Matthew and Melangell, hemmed in among the jostling, singing, jubilant train. Somewhere along that half-mile of road they were caught up in the fever and joy of the day, borne along on the tide of music and devotion, forgetting all others, forgetting even themselves, drawn into one without any word or motion of theirs. When they turned their heads to look at each other, they saw only mated eyes and a halo of sunshine. They did not speak at all, not once along the way. They had no need of speech. But when they had turned the corner of the precinct wall by the horse-fair, and drew near to the gatehouse, and heard and saw the abbot leading his own party out to meet them, splendidly vested and immensely tall under his mitre; when the two chants found their measure while yet some way apart, and met and married in a triumphant, soaring cry of worship, and all the ardent followers drew gasping breaths of exultation, Melangell heard beside her a broken breath drawn, like a soft sob, that turned as suddenly into a peal of laughter, out of pure, possessed joy. Not a loud sound, muted and short of breath because the throat that uttered it was clenched by emotion, and the mind and heart from which it came quite unaware of what it shed upon the world. It was a beautiful sound, or so Melangell thought, as she raised her head to stare at him with wide eyes and parted lips, in dazzled and dazzling delight. Matthew's wry and rare smile she had seen sometimes, and wondered and grieved at its brevity, but never before had she heard him laugh.

The two processions merged. The cross-bearers walked before, Abbot Radulfus, prior and choir monks came after, and Cadfael and his peers with their sacred burden followed, hemmed in on both sides by worshippers who reached and leaned to touch even the sleeve of a bearer's habit, or the polished oak of the reliquary as it passed. Brother Anselm, in secure command of his choir, raised his own fine voice in the lead as they turned in at the gatehouse, bringing Saint Winifred home.

Brother Cadfael, by then, was moving like a man in a dual dream, his body keeping pace and time with his fellows, in one confident rhythm, while his mind soared in another, carried aloft on the cushioned cloud of sounds, compounded of the eager footsteps, exalted murmurs and shrill acclamations of hundreds of people, with the chant borne above it, and the voice of Brother Anselm soaring over all. The great court was crowded with people to watch them enter, the way into the cloister, and so into the church, had to be cleared by slow, shuffling paces, the ranks pressing back to give them passage, Cadfael came to himself with some mild annoyance when the reliquary was halted in the court, to wait for a clear path ahead. He braced both feet almost aggressively into the familiar soil, and for the first time looked about him. He saw, beyond the throng already gathered, the saint's own retinue melting and flowing to find a place where eye might see all, and ear hear all. In this brief halt he saw Melangell and Matthew, hand in hand, hunt round the fringes of the crowd, and find a place to gaze.

They looked to Cadfael a little tipsy, like unaccustomed drinkers after strong wine. And why not? After long abstention he had felt the intoxication possessing his own feet, as they held the hypnotic rhythm, and his own mind, as it floated on the cadences of song. Those ecstasies were at once native and alien to him, he could both embrace and stand clear of them, feet firmly planted, gripping the homely earth, to keep his balance and stand erect.

They moved forward again into the nave of the church, and then to the right, towards the bared and waiting altar. The vast, dreaming, sun-warmed bulk of the church enclosed them, dim, silent and empty, since no other could enter until they had discharged their duty, lodged their patroness and retired to their own insignificant places. Then they came, led by abbot and prior, first the brothers to fill up their stalls in the choir, then the provost and guildsmen of the town and the notables of the shire, and then all that great concourse of people, flooding in from hot mid-morning sunlight to the cool dimness of stone, and from the excited clamour of festival to the great silence of worship, until all the space of the nave was filled with the colour and warmth and breath of humanity, and all as still as the candle-flames on the altar. Even the reflected gleams in the silver chacings of the casket were fixed and motionless as jewels.

Abbot Radulfus stood forth. The sobering solemnity of the Mass began.

For the very intensity of all that mortal emotion gathered thus between confining walls and beneath one roof, it was impossible to withdraw the eyes for an instant from the act of worship on which it was centred, or the mind from the words of the office. There had been times, through the years of his vocation, when Cadfael's thoughts had strayed during Mass to worrying at other problems, and working out other intents. It was not so now. Throughout, he was unaware of a single face in all that throng, only of the presence of humankind, in whom his own identity was lost;

164

or, perhaps, into whom his own identity expanded like air, to fill every part of the whole. He forgot Melangell and Matthew, he forgot Ciaran and Rhun, he never looked round to see if Hugh had come. If there was a face before his mind's eye at all it was one he had never seen, though he well remembered the slight and fragile bones he had lifted with such care and awe out of the earth, and with so much better heart again laid beneath the same soil, there to resume her hawthorn-scented sleep under the sheltering trees. For some reason, though she had lived to a good old age, he could not imagine her older than seventeen or eighteen, as she had been when the king's son Cradoc pursued her. The slender little bones had cried out of youth, and the shadowy face he had imagined for her was fresh and eager and open, and very beautiful. But he saw it always half turned away from him. Now, if ever, she might at last look round, and show him fully that reassuring countenance.

At the end of Mass the abbot withdrew to his own stall, to the right of the entrance from nave to choir, round the parish altar, and with lifted voice and open arms bade the pilgrims advance to the saint's altar, where everyone who had a petition to make might make it on his knees, and touch the reliquary with hand and lip. And in orderly and reverent silence they came. Prior Robert took his stand at the foot of the three steps that led up to the altar, ready to offer a hand to those who needed help to mount or kneel. Those who were in health and had no pressing requirements to advance came through from the nave on the other side, and found corners where they might stand and watch, and miss nothing of this memorable day. They had faces again, they spoke in whispers, they were as various as an hour since they had been one.

On his knees in his stall, Brother Cadfael looked on, knowing them one from another now as they came, kneeled and touched. The long file of petitioners was drawing near its end when he saw Rhun approaching. Dame Alice had a hand solicitously under his left elbow, Melangell nursed him along on his right, Matthew followed close, no less anxious than they. The boy advanced with his usual laborious gait, his dragging toe just scraping the tiles of the floor. His face was intensely pale, but with a brilliant pallor that almost dazzled the watching eyes, and the wide gaze he fixed steadily upon the reliquary shone translucent, like ice with a bright bluish light behind it. Dame Alice was whispering low, encouraging entreaties into one ear, Melangell into the other, but he was aware of nothing but the altar towards which he moved. When his turn came, he shook off his supporters, and for a moment seemed to hesitate before venturing to advance alone.

Prior Robert observed his condition, and

held out a hand. 'You need not be abashed, my son, because you cannot kneel. God and the saint will know your goodwill.'

The softest whisper of a voice, though clearly audible in the waiting silence, said tremulously: 'But, Father, I can! I will!'

Rhun straightened up, taking his hands from his crutches, which slid from under his armpits and fell. That on the left crashed with an unnerving clatter upon the tiles, on the right Melangell started forward and dropped to her knees, catching the falling prop in her arms with a faint cry. And there she crouched, embracing the discarded thing desperately, while Rhun set his twisted foot to the ground and stood upright. He had but two or three paces to go to the foot of the altar steps. He took them slowly and steadily, his eyes fixed upon the reliquary. Once he lurched slightly, and Dame Alice made a trembling move to run after him, only to halt again in wonder and fear, while Prior Robert again extended his hand to offer aid. Rhun paid no attention to them or to anyone else, he did not seem to see or hear anything but his goal, and whatever voice it might be that called him forward. For he went with held breath, as a child learning to walk ventures across perilous distances to reach its mother's open arms and coaxing, praising blandishments that wooed it to the deed.

It was the twisted foot he set first on the

lowest step, and now the twisted foot, though a little awkward and unpractised, was twisted no longer, and did not fail him, and the wasted leg, as he put his weight on it, seemed to have smoothed out into shapeliness, and bore him up bravely.

Only then did Cadfael become aware of the stillness and the silence, as if every soul present held his breath with the boy, spellbound, not yet ready, not yet permitted to acknowledge what they saw before their eyes. Even Prior Robert stood charmed into a tall, austere statue, frozen at gaze. Even Melangell, crouching with the crutch hugged to her breast, could not stir a finger to help or break the spell, but hung upon every deliberate step with agonised eyes, as though she were laying her heart under his feet as a voluntary sacrifice to buy off fate.

He had reached the third step, he sank to his knees with only the gentlest of manipulations, holding by the fringes of the altar frontal, and the cloth of gold that was draped under the reliquary. He lifted his joined hands and starry face, white and bright even with eyes now closed, and though there was hardly any sound they saw his lips moving upon whatever prayers he had made ready for her. Certainly they contained no request for his own healing. He had put himself simply in her hands, submissively and joyfully, and what had been done to him and for him surely she had done, of her own perfect will.

He had to hold by her draperies to rise, as babes hold by their mothers' skirts. No doubt but she had him under the arms to raise him. He bent his fair head and kissed the hem of her garment, rose erect and kissed the silver rim of the reliquary, in which, whether she lay or not, she alone commanded and had sovereignty. Then he withdrew from her, feeling his way backward down the three steps. Twisted foot and shrunken leg carried him securely. At the foot he made obeisance gravely, and then turned and went briskly, like any other healthy lad of sixteen, to smile reassurance on his trembling womenfolk, take up gently the crutches for which he had no further use, and carry them back to lay them tidily under the altar.

The spell broke, for the marvellous thing was done, and its absolute nature made manifest. A great, shuddering sigh went round nave, choir, transepts and all, wherever there were human creatures watching and listening. And after the sigh the quivering murmur of a gathering storm, whether of tears or laughter there was no telling, but the air shook with its passion. And then the outcry, the loosing of both tears and laughter, in a gale of wonder and praise. From stone walls and lofty, arched roof, from rood-loft and transept arcades, the echoes flew and rebounded, and the candles that had stood so still and tall shook and guttered in the gale. Melangell hung weak with weeping and joy in Matthew's arms, Dame Alice whirled from friend to friend, spouting tears like a fountain, and smiling like the most blessed of women. Prior Robert lifted his hands in vindicated stewardship, and his voice in the opening of a thanksgiving psalm, and Brother Anselm took up the chant.

A miracle, a miracle, a miracle . . .

And in the midst Rhun stood erect and still, even a little bewildered, braced sturdily on his two long, shapely legs, looking all about him at the shouting, weeping, exulting faces, letting the meaningless sounds wash over him in waves, wanting the quiet he had known when there had been no one here in this holy place but himself and his saint, who had told him, in how sweet and private conference, all that he had to do.

*   *   *

Brother Cadfael rose with his brothers, after the church was cleared of all others, after all that jubilant, bubbling, boiling throng had gone forth to spill its feverish excitement in open summer air, to cry the miracle aloud, carry it out into the Foregate, beyond into the town, buffet it back and forth across the tables at dinner in the guest-hall, and return to extol it at Vespers with what breath was left. When they dispersed the word would go with them wherever they went, sounding Saint Winifred's praises, inspiring other souls to take to the roads and bring their troubles to Shrewsbury. Where healing was proven, and attested by hundreds of voices.

The brothers went to their modest, accustomed dinner in the refectory, and observed, whatever their own feelings were, the discipline of silence. They were very tired, which made silence welcome. They had risen early, worked hard, been through fire and flood body and soul, no wonder they ate humbly, thankfully, in silence.

CHAPTER TEN

It was not until dinner was almost over in the guest-hall that Matthew, seated at Melangell's side and still flushed and exalted from the morning's heady wonders, suddenly bethought him of sterner matters, and began to look back with a thoughtful frown which as yet only faintly dimmed the unaccustomed brightness of his face. Being in attendance on Mistress Weaver and her young people had made him a part, for a while, of their unshadowed joy, and caused him to forget everything else. But it could not last, though Rhun sat there half-lost in wonder still, with hardly a word to say, and felt no need of food or drink, and his womenfolk fawned on him unregarded. So far away had he been that the return took time.

'I haven't seen Ciaran,' said Matthew quietly in Melangell's ear, and he rose a little in his place to look round the crowded room. 'Did you catch ever a glimpse of him in the church?'

She, too, had forgotten until then, but at sight of his face she remembered all too sharply, with a sickening lurch of her heart. But she kept her countenance, and laid a persuasive hand on his arm to draw him down again beside her. 'Among so many? But he surely would be there. He must have been among the first, he stayed here, he would find a good place. We didn't see all those who went to the altar—we all stayed with Rhun, and his place was far back.' Such a mingling of truth and lies, but she kept her voice confident, and clung to her shaken hope.

'But where is he now? I don't see him within here.' Though there was so much excitement, so much moving about from table to table to talk with friends, that one man might easily avoid detection. 'I must find him,' said Matthew, not yet greatly troubled but wanting reassurance, and rose.

'No, sit down! You know he must be here somewhere. Let him alone, and he'll appear when he chooses. He may be resting on his bed, if he has to go forth again barefoot tomorrow. Why look for him now? Can you not do without him even one day? And such a day?'

Matthew looked down at her with a face from which all the openness and joy had faded, and freed his sleeve from her grasp gently enough, but decidedly. 'Still, I must find him. Stay here with Rhun, I'll come back. All I want is to see him, to be sure . . .'

He was away, slipping quietly out between the festive tables, looking sharply about him as he went. She was in two minds about following him, but then she thought better of it, for while he hunted time would be slipping softly away, and Ciaran would be dwindling into distance, as later she prayed he could fade even out of mind, and be forgotten. So she remained with the happy company, but not of it, and with every passing moment hesitated whether to grow more reassured or more uneasy. At last she could not bear the waiting any longer. She rose quietly and slipped away. Dame Alice was in full spate, torn between tears and smiles, sitting proudly by her prodigy, and surrounded by neighbours as happy and voluble as herself, and Rhun, still somehow apart though he was the centre of the group, sat withdrawn into his revelation, even as he answered eager questions, lamely enough but as well as he could. They had no need of Melangell, they would not miss her for a little while.

When she came out into the great court, into the brilliance of the noonday sun, it was

173

the quietest hour, the pause after meat. There never was a time of day when there was no traffic about the court, no going and coming at the gatehouse, but now it moved at its gentlest and quietest. She went down almost fearfully into the cloister, and found no one there but a single copyist busy reviewing what he had done the previous day, and Brother Anselm in his workshop going over the music for Vespers; into the stable-yard, though there was no reason in the world why Matthew should be there, having no mount, and no expectation that his companion would or possibly could acquire one; into the gardens, where a couple of novices were clipping back the too exuberant shoots of a box hedge; even into the grange court, where the barns and storehouses were, and a few lay servants were taking their ease, and harrowing over the morning's marvel, like everyone else within the enclave, and most of Shrewsbury and the Foregate into the bargain. The abbot's garden was empty, neat, glowing with carefully-tended roses, his lodging showed an open door, and some ordered bustle of guests within.

She turned back towards the garden, now in deep anxiety. She was not good at lying, she had no practice, even for a good end she could not but botch the effort. And for all the to and fro of customary commerce within the pale, never without work to be done, she had seen nothing of Matthew. But he could not be gone, no, the porter could tell him nothing, Ciaran had not passed there; and she would not, never until she must, never until Matthew's too fond heart was reconciled to loss, and open and receptive to a better gain.

She turned back, rounding the box hedge and out of sight of the busy novices, and walked breast to breast into Matthew.

They met between the thick hedges, in a terrible privacy. She started back from him in a brief revulsion of guilt, for he looked more distant and alien than ever before, even as he recognised her, and acknowledged with a contortion of his troubled face her right to come out in search of him, and almost in the same instant frowned her off as irrelevant.

'He's gone!' he said in a chill and grating voice, and looked through her and far beyond. 'God keep you, Melangell, you must fend for yourself now, sorry as I am. He's gone—fled while my back was turned. I've looked for him everywhere, and never a trace of him. Nor has the porter seen him pass the gate, I've asked there. But he's gone! Alone! And I must go after him. God keep you, girl, as I cannot, and fare you well!'

And he was going so, with so few words and so cold and wild a face! He had turned on his heel and taken two long steps before she flung herself after him, caught him by the arms in both hands, and dragged him to a halt.

'No, no, *why*? What need has he of you, to

175

match with my need? He's gone? Let him go! Do you think your life belongs to him? He doesn't want it! He wants you free, he wants you to live your own life, not die his death with him. He knows, he knows you love me! Dare you deny it? He knows I love you. He wants you happy! Why should not a friend want his friend to be happy? Who are you to deny him his last wish?'

She knew by then that she had said too much, but never knew at what point the error had become mortal. He had turned fully to her again, and frozen where he stood, and his face was like chiselled marble. He tugged his sleeve out of her grasp this time with no gentleness at all.

'*He wants!*' hissed a voice she had never heard before, driven through narrowed lips. 'You've spoken with him! You speak *for* him! *You knew!* You knew he meant to go, and leave me here bewitched, damned, false to my oath. *You knew!* When? When did you speak with him?'

He had her by the wrists, he shook her mercilessly, and she cried out and fell to her knees.

'You knew he meant to go?' persisted Matthew, stooping over her in a cold frenzy.

'Yes—yes! This morning he told me . . . he wished it . . .'

'*He wished it!* How dared he wish it? How could he dare, robbed of his bishop's ring as he was? He dared not stir without it, he was terrified to set foot outside the pale . . .'

'He has the ring,' she cried, abandoning all deceit. 'The lord abbot gave it back to him this morning, you need not fret for him, he's safe enough, he has his protection . . . He doesn't need you!'

Matthew had fallen into a deadly stillness, stooping above her. *'He has the ring?* And you knew it, and never said word! If you know so much, how much more do you know. Speak! *Where is he?'*

'Gone,' she said in a trembling whisper, 'and wished you well, wished us both well . . . wished us to be happy . . . Oh, let him go, let him go, he sets you free!'

Something that was certainly a laugh convulsed Matthew, she heard it with her ears and felt it shiver through her flesh, but it was like no other laughter she had ever heard, it chilled her blood. *'He* sets *me* free! And you must be his confederate! Oh, God! He never passed the gate. If you know all, then tell all— how did he go?'

She faltered, weeping: 'He loved you, he willed you to live and forget him, and be happy . . .'

'How did he go?' repeated Matthew, in a voice so ill-supplied with breath it seemed he might strangle on the words.

'Across the brook,' she said in a broken whisper, 'making the quickest way for Wales.

177

He said . . . he has kin there . . .'

He drew in hissing breath and took his hands from her, leaving her drooping forward on her face as he let go of her wrists. He had turned his back and flung away from her, all they had shared forgotten, his obsession plucking him away. She did not understand, there was no way she could come to terms so rapidly with all that had happened, but she knew she had loosed her hold of her love, and he was in merciless flight from her in pursuit of some incomprehensible duty in which she had no part and no right. She sprang up and ran after him, caught him by the arm, wound her own arms about him, lifted her imploring face to his stony, frantic stare, and prayed him passionately: 'Let him go! Oh, let him go! He wants to go alone and leave you to me . . .'

Almost silently above her the terrible laughter, so opposed to that lovely sound as he followed the reliquary with her, boiled like some thick, choking syrup in his throat. He struggled to shake off her clinging hands, and when she fell to her knees again and hung upon him with all her despairing weight he tore loose his right hand, and struck her heavily in the face, sobbing, and so wrenched himself loose and fled, leaving her face-down on the ground.

*   *   *

In the abbot's lodging Radulfus and his guests sat long over their meal, for they had much to discuss. The topic which was on everyone's lips naturally came first.

'It would seem,' said the abbot, 'that we have been singularly favoured this morning. Certain motions of grace we have seen before, but never yet one so public and so persuasive, with so many witnesses. How do you say? I grow old in experience of wonders, some of which turn out to fall somewhat short of their promise. I know of human deception, not always deliberate, for sometimes the deceiver is himself deceived. If saints have power, so have demons. Yet this boy seems to me as crystal. I cannot think he either cheats or is cheated.'

'I have heard,' said Hugh, 'of cripples who discarded their crutches and walked without them, only to relapse when the fervour of the occasion was over. Time will prove whether this one takes to his crutches again.'

'I shall speak with him later,' said the abbot, 'after the excitement has cooled. I hear from Brother Edmund that Brother Cadfael has been treating the boy these three days he has been here. That may have eased his condition, but it can scarcely have brought about so sudden a cure. No, I must say it, I truly believe our house has been the happy scene of divine grace. I will speak also with Cadfael, who must know the boy's condition.'

Olivier sat quiet and deferential in the presence of so reverend a churchman as the abbot, but Hugh observed that his arched lids lifted and his eyes kindled at Cadfael's name. So he knew who it was he sought, and something more than a distant salute in action had passed between that strangely assorted pair.

'And now I should be glad,' said the abbot, 'to hear what news you bring from the south. Have you been in Westminster with the empress's court? For I hear she is now installed there.'

Olivier gave his account of affairs in London readily, and answered questions with goodwill. 'My lord has remained in Oxford, it was at his wish I undertook this errand. I was not in London, I set out from Winchester. But the empress is in the palace of Westminster, and the plans for her coronation go forward—admittedly very slowly. The city of London is well aware of its power, and means to exact due recognition of it, or so it seems to me.' He would go no nearer than that to voicing whatever qualms he felt about his liege lady's wisdom or want of it, but he jutted a dubious underlip, and momentarily frowned. 'Father, you were there at the council, you know all that happened. My lord lost a good knight there, and I a valued friend, struck down in the street.'

'Rainald Bossard,' said Radulfus sombrely.

180

'I have not forgotten.'

'Father, I have been telling the lord sheriff here what I should like to tell also to you. For I have a second errand to pursue, wherever I go on the business of the empress, an errand for Rainald's widow. Rainald had a young kinsman in his household, who was with him when he was killed, and after that death this young man left the lady's service without a word, secretly. She says he had grown closed and silent even before he vanished, and the only trace of him afterwards was on the road to Newbury, going north. Since then, nothing. So knowing I was bound north, she begged me to enquire for him wherever I came, for she values and trusts him, and needs him at her side. I may not deceive you, Father, there are those who say he has fled because he is guilty of Rainald's death. They claim he was besotted with Dame Juliana, and may have seized his chance in this brawl to widow her, and get her for himself, and then taken fright because these things were so soon being said. But *I* think they were not being said at all until after he had vanished. And Juliana, who surely knows him better than any, and looks upon him as a son, for want of children of her own, she is quite sure of him. She wants him home and vindicated, for whatever reason he left her as he did. And I have been asking at every lodging and monastery along the road for word of such a young man. May I also ask here? Brother Hospitaller will know the names of all his guests. Though a name,' he added ruefully, 'is almost all I have, for if ever I saw the man it was without knowing it was he. And the name he may have left behind him.'

'It is not much to go on,' said Abbot Radulfus with a smile, 'but certainly you may enquire. If he has done no wrong, I should be glad to help you to find him and bring him off without reproach. What is his name?'

'Luc Meverel. Twenty-four years old, they tell me, middling tall and well made, dark of hair and eye.'

'It could fit many hundreds of young men,' said the abbot, shaking his head, 'and the name I doubt he will have put off if he has anything to hide, or even if he fears it may be unfairly besmirched. Yet try. I grant you in such a gathering as we have here now a young man who wished to be lost might bury himself very thoroughly. Denis will know which of his guests is of the right age and quality. For clearly your Luc Meverel is well-born, and most likely tutored and lettered.'

'Certainly so,' said Olivier.

'Then by all means, and with my blessing, go freely to Brother Denis, and see what he can do to help you. He has an excellent memory, he will be able to tell you which, among the men here, is of suitable years, and gentle. You can but try.'

*   *   *

On leaving the lodging they went first,
however, to look for Brother Cadfael. And
Brother Cadfael was not so easily found.
Hugh's first resort was the workshop in the
herbarium, where they habitually compounded
their affairs. But there was no Cadfael there.
Nor was he with Brother Anselm in the
cloister, where he well might have been
debating some nice point in the evening's
music. Nor checking the medicine cupboard in
the infirmary, which must surely have been
depleted during these last few days, but had
clearly been restocked in the early hours of
this day of glory. Brother Edmund said mildly:
'He was here. I had a poor soul who bled from
the mouth—too gorged, I think, with devotion.
But he's quiet and sleeping now, the flux has
stopped. Cadfael went away some while since.'

Brother Oswin, vigorously fighting weeds in
the kitchen garden, had not seen his superior
since dinner. 'But I think,' he said, blinking
thoughtfully into the sun in the zenith, 'he may
be in the church.'

*   *   *

Cadfael was on his knees at the foot of Saint
Winifred's three-tread stairway to grace, his
hands not lifted in prayer but folded in the lap
of his habit, his eyes not closed in entreaty but

wide open to absolution. He had been kneeling there for some time, he who was usually only too glad to rise from knees now perceptibly stiffening. He felt no pains, no griefs of any kind, nothing but an immense thankfulness in which he floated like a fish in an ocean. An ocean as pure and blue and drowningly deep and clear as that well-remembered eastern sea, the furthest extreme of the tideless midland sea of legend, at the end of which lay the holy city of Jerusalem, Our Lord's burial-place and hard-won kingdom. The saint who presided here, whether she lay here or no, had launched him into a shining infinity of hope. Her mercies might be whimsical, they were certainly magisterial. She had reached her hand to an innocent, well deserving her kindness. What had she intended towards this less innocent but no less needy being?

Behind him, approaching quietly from the nave, a known voice said softly: 'And are you demanding yet a second miracle?'

He withdrew his eyes reluctantly from the reflected gleams of silver along the reliquary, and turned to look towards the parish altar. He saw the expected shape of Hugh Beringar, the thin dark face smiling at him. But over Hugh's shoulder he saw a taller head and shoulders loom, emerging from dimness in suave, resplendent planes, the bright, jutting cheekbones, the olive cheeks smoothly hollowed below, the falcon's amber eyes beneath high-arched black brows, the long, supple lips tentatively smiling upon him.

It was not possible. Yet he beheld it. Olivier de Bretagne came out of the shadows and stepped unmistakable into the light of the altar candles. And that was the moment when Saint Winifred turned her head, looked fully into the face of her fallible but faithful servant, and also smiled.

A second miracle! Why not? When she gave she gave prodigally, with both hands.

CHAPTER ELEVEN

They went out into the cloister all three together, and that in itself was memorable and good, for they had never been together before. Those trusting intimacies which had once passed between Cadfael and Olivier, on a winter night in Bromfield priory, were unknown still to Hugh, and there was a mysterious constraint still that prevented Olivier from openly recalling them. The greetings they exchanged were warm but brief, only the reticence behind them was eloquent, and no doubt Hugh understood that well enough, and was willing to wait for enlightenment, or courteously to make do without it. For that there was no haste, but for

Luc Meverel there might be.

'Our friend has a quest,' said Hugh, 'in which we mean to enlist Brother Denis's help, but we shall also be very glad of yours. He is looking for a young man by the name of Luc Meverel, strayed from his place and known to be travelling north. Tell him the way of it, Olivier.'

Olivier told the story over again, and was listened to with close attention. 'Very gladly,' said Cadfael then, 'would I do whatever man can do not only to bring off an innocent man from such a charge, but also to bring the charge home to the guilty. We know of this murder, and it sticks in every gullet that a decent man, protecting his honourable opponent, should be cut down by one of his own faction . . .'

'Is that certain?' wondered Hugh sharply.

'As good as certain. Who else would so take exception to the man standing up for his lady and doing his errand without fear? All who still held to Stephen in their hearts would approve, even if they dared not applaud him. And as for a chance attack by sneak-thieves— why choose to prey on a mere clerk, with nothing of value on him but the simple needs of his journey, when the town was full of nobles, clerics and merchants far better worth robbing? Rainald died only because he came to the clerk's aid. No, an adherent of the empress, like Rainald himself but most unlike,

186

committed that infamy.'

'That's good sense,' agreed Olivier. 'But my chief concern now is to find Luc, and send him home again if I can.'

'There must be twenty or more young fellows in that age here today,' said Cadfael, scrubbing thoughtfully at his blunt brown nose, 'but I dare wager most of them can be pricked out of the list as well known to some of their companions by their own right names, or by reason of their calling or condition. Solitaries may come, but they're few and far between. Pilgrims are like starlings, they thrive on company. We'd best go and talk to Brother Denis. He'll have sorted out most of them by now.'

Brother Denis had a retentive memory and an appetite for news and rumours that usually kept him the best-informed person in the enclave. The fuller his halls, the more pleasure he took in knowing everything that went on there, and the name and vocation of every guest. He also kept meticulous books to record the visitations.

They found him in the narrow cell where he kept his accounts and estimated his future needs, thoughtfully reckoning up what provisions he still had, and how rapidly the demands on them were likely to dwindle from the morrow. He took his mind from his store-book courteously in order to listen to what Brother Cadfael and the sheriff required of him, and produced answers with exemplary promptitude when asked to sieve out from his swollen household males of about twenty-five years, bred gentle or within modest reach of gentility, lettered, of dark colouring and medium tall build, answering to the very bare description of Luc Meverel. As his forefinger flew down the roster of his guests the numbers shrank remarkably. It seemed to be true that considerably more than half of those who went on pilgrimage were women, and that among the men the greater part were in their forties or fifties, and of those remaining, many would be in minor orders, either monastics or secular priests or would-be priests. And Luc Meverel was none of these.

'Are there any here,' asked Hugh, viewing the final list, which was short enough, 'who came solitary?'

Brother Denis cocked his round, rosy, tonsured head aside and ran a sharp brown eye, very reminiscent of a robin's, down the list. 'Not one. Young squires of that age seldom go as pilgrims, unless with an exigent lord—or an equally exigent lady. In such a summer feast as this we might have young friends coming together, to take the fill of the time before they settle down to sterner disciplines. But alone ... Where would be the pastime in that?'

'Here are two, at any rate,' said Cadfael, 'who came together, but surely not for pastime. They have puzzled me, I own. Both are of the proper age, and such word as we have of the man we're looking for would fit either. You know them, Denis—that youngster who's on his way to Aberdaron, and his friend who bears him company. Both lettered, both bred to the manor. And certainly they came from the south, beyond Abingdon, according to Brother Adam of Reading, who lodged there the same night.'

'Ah, the barefoot traveller,' said Denis, and laid a finger on Ciaran in the shrunken toll of young men, 'and his keeper and worshipper. Yes, I would not put half a year between them, and they have the build and colouring, but you needed only one.'

'We could at least look at two,' said Cadfael. 'If neither of them is what we're seeking, yet coming from that region they may have encountered such a single traveller somewhere on the road. If we have not the authority to question them closely about who they are and whence they come, and how and why thus linked, then Father Abbot has. And if they have no reason to court concealment, then they'll willingly declare to him what they might not as readily utter to us.'

'We may try it,' said Hugh, kindling. 'At least it's worth the asking, and if they have nothing to do with the man we are looking for, neither they nor we have lost more than half an hour of time, and surely they won't grudge us that.'

'Granted what is so far related of these two hardly fits the case,' Cadfael acknowledged doubtfully, 'for the one is said to be mortally ill and going to Aberdaron to die, and the other is resolute to keep him company to the end. But a young man who wishes to disappear may provide himself with a circumstantial story as easily as with a new name. And at all events, between Abingdon and Shrewsbury it's possible they may have encountered Luc Meverel alone and under his own name.'

'But if one of these two, either of these two, should truly be the man I want,' said Olivier doubtfully, 'then who, in the name of God, is the other?'

'We ask each other questions,' said Hugh practically, 'which either of these two could answer in a moment. Come, let's leave Abbot Radulfus to call them in, and see what comes of it.'

*   *   *

It was not difficult to induce the abbot to have the two young men sent for. It was not so easy to find them and bring them to speak for themselves. The messenger, sent forth in expectation of prompt obedience, came back after a much longer time than had been expected, and reported ruefully that neither of the pair could be found within the abbey walls. True, the porter had not actually seen either of them pass the gatehouse. But what had satisfied him that the two were leaving was that the young man Matthew had come, no long time after dinner, to reclaim his dagger, and had left behind him a generous gift of money to the house, saying that he and his friend were already bound away on their journey, and desired to offer thanks for their lodging. And had he seemed—it was Cadfael who asked it, himself hardly knowing why— had he seemed as he always was, or in any way disturbed or alarmed or out of countenance and temper, when he came for his weapon and paid his and his friend's score?

The messenger shook his head, having asked no such question at the gate. Brother Porter, when enquiry was made direct by Cadfael himself, said positively: 'He was like a man on fire. Oh, as soft as ever in voice, and courteous, but pale and alight, you'd have said his hair stood on end. But what with every soul within here wandering in a dream, since this wonder, I never thought but here were some going forth with the news while the furnace was still white-hot.'

'Gone?' said Olivier, dismayed, when this word was brought back to the abbot's parlour. 'Now I begin to see better cause why one of these two, for all they come so strangely paired, and so strangely account for themselves, may be the man I'm seeking. For if I do not know Luc Meverel by sight, I have been two or three times his lord's guest recently, and he may well have taken note of me. How if he saw me come, today, and is gone hence thus in haste because he does not wish to be found? He could hardly know I am sent to look for him, but he might, for all that, prefer to put himself clean out of sight. And an ailing companion on the way would be good cover for a man wanting a reason for his wanderings. I wish I might yet speak with these two. How long have they been gone?'

'It cannot have been more than an hour and a half after noon,' said Cadfael, 'according to when Matthew reclaimed his dagger.'

'And afoot!' Olivier kindled hopefully. 'And even unshod, the one of them! It should be no great labour to overtake them, if it's known what road they will have taken.'

'By far their best way is by the Oswestry road, and so across the dyke into Wales. According to Brother Denis, that was Ciaran's declared intent.'

'Then, Father Abbot,' said Olivier eagerly, 'with your leave I'll mount and ride after them, for they cannot have got far. It would be a pity to miss the chance, and even if they are not what I'm seeking, neither they nor I will have lost anything. But with or without my man, I shall return here.'

'I'll ride through the town with you,' said Hugh, 'and set you on your way, for this will be new country to you. But then I must be about my own business, and see if we've gathered any harvest from this morning's hunt. I doubt they've gone deeper into the forest, or I should have had word by now. We shall look for you back before night, Olivier. One more night at the least we mean to keep you and longer if we can.'

Olivier took his leave hastily but gracefully, made a dutiful reverence to the abbot, and turned upon Brother Cadfael a brief, radiant smile that shattered his preoccupation for an instant like a sunburst through clouds. 'I will not leave here,' he said in simple reassurance, 'without having quiet conference with you. But this I must see finished, if I can.'

They were gone away briskly to the stables, where they had left their horses before Mass. Abbot Radulfus looked after them with a very thoughtful face.

'Do you find it surprising, Cadfael, that these two young pilgrims should leave so soon, and so abruptly? Is it possible the coming of Messire de Bretagne can have driven them away?'

Cadfael considered, and shook his head. 'No, I think not. In the great press this morning, and the excitement, why should one man among the many be noticed, and one not looked for at all in these parts? But, yes, their going does greatly surprise me. For the one, he should surely be only too glad of an extra day or two of rest before taking barefoot to the roads again. And for the other—Father, there is a girl he certainly admires and covets, whether he yet knows it to the full or no, and with her he spent this morning, following Saint Winifred home, and I am certain there was then no other thought in his mind but of her and her kin, and the greatness of this day. For she is sister to the boy Rhun, who came by so great a mercy and blessing before our eyes. It would take some very strong compulsion to drag him away suddenly like this.'

'The boy's sister, you say?' Abbot Radulfus recalled an intent which had been shelved in favour of Olivier's quest. 'There is still an hour or more before Vespers. I should like to talk with this youth. You have been treating his condition, Cadfael. Do you think your handling has had anything to do with what we witnessed today? Or could he—though I would not willingly attribute falsity to one so young—could he have made more of his distress than it was, in order to produce a prodigy?'

'No,' said Cadfael very decidedly. 'There is no deceit at all in him. And as for my poor skills, they might in a long time of perseverance have softened the tight cords that hampered the use of his limb, and made it possible to set a little weight on it—but straighten that foot and fill out the sinews of the leg—never! The greatest doctor in the world could not have done it. Father, on the day he came I gave him a draught that should have eased his pain and brought him sleep.

194

After three nights he sent it back to me untouched. He saw no reason why he should expect to be singled out for healing, but he said that he offered his pain freely, who had nothing else to give. Not to buy grace, but of his goodwill to give and want nothing in return. And further, it seems that thus having accepted his pain out of love, his pain left him. After Mass we saw that deliverance completed.'

'Then it was well deserved,' said Radulfus, pleased and moved. 'I must indeed talk with this boy. Will you find him for me, Cadfael, and bring him here to me now?'

'Very gladly, Father,' said Cadfael, and departed on his errand. Dame Alice was sitting in the sunshine of the cloister garth, the centre of a voluble circle of other matrons, her face so bright with the joy of the day that it warmed the very air; but Rhun was not with them. Melangell had withdrawn into the shadow of the arcade, as though the light was too bright for her eyes, and kept her face averted over the mending of a frayed seam in a linen shirt which must belong to her brother. Even when Cadfael addressed her she looked up only very swiftly and timidly, and again stooped into shadow, but even in that glimpse he saw that the joy which had made her shine like a new rose in the morning was dimmed and pale now in the lengthening afternoon. And was he merely imagining that her left cheek showed the faint bluish tint of a bruise? But at the mention of Rhun's name she smiled, as though at the recollection of happiness rather than its presence.

'He said he was tired, and went away into the dortoir to rest. Aunt Weaver thinks he is lying down on his bed, but I think he wanted only to be left alone, to be quiet and not have to talk. He is tired by having to answer things he seems not to understand himself.'

'He speaks another tongue today from the rest of mankind,' said Cadfael. 'It may well be we who don't understand, and ask things that have no meaning for him.' He took her gently by the chin and turned her face up to the light, but she twisted nervously out of his hold. 'You have hurt yourself?' Certainly it was a bruise beginning there.

'It's nothing,' she said. 'My own fault. I was in the garden, I ran too fast and I fell. I know it's unsightly, but it doesn't hurt now.'

Her eyes were very calm, not reddened, only a little swollen as to the lids. Well, Matthew had gone, abandoned her to go with his friend, letting her fall only too disastrously after the heady running together of the morning hours. That could account for tears now past. But should it account for a bruised cheek? He hesitated whether to question further, but clearly she did not wish it. She had gone back doggedly to her work, and would not look up again.

Cadfael sighed, and went out across the

great court to the guest-hall. Even a glorious day like this one must have its vein of bitter sadness.

In the men's dortoir Rhun sat alone on his bed, very still and content in his blissfully restored body. He was deep in his own rapt thoughts, but readily aware when Cadfael entered. He looked round and smiled.

'Brother, I was wishing to see you. You were there, you know. Perhaps you even heard . . . See, how I'm changed!' The leg once maimed stretched out perfect before him, he bent and stamped the boards of the floor. He flexed ankle and toes, drew up his knee to his chin, and everything moved as smoothly and painlessly as his ready tongue. 'I am whole! I never asked it, how dared I? Even then, I was praying not for this, and yet this was given . . .' He went away again for a moment into his tranced dream.

Cadfael sat down beside him, noting the exquisite fluency of those joints hitherto flawed and intransigent. The boy's beauty was perfected now.

'You were praying,' said Cadfael gently, 'for Melangell.'

'Yes. And Matthew, too. I truly thought . . . But you see he is gone. They are both gone, gone together. Why could I not bring my sister into bliss? I would have gone on crutches all my life for that, but I couldn't prevail.'

'That is not yet determined,' said Cadfael

197

firmly. 'Who goes may also return. And I think your prayers should have strong virtue, if you do not fall into doubt now, because heaven has need of a little time. Even miracles have their times. Half our lives in this world are spent in waiting. It is needful to wait with faith.'

Rhun sat listening with an absent smile, and at the end of it he said: 'Yes, surely, and I will wait. For see, one of them left this behind in his haste when he went away.'

He reached down between the close-set cots, and lifted to the bed between them a bulky but lightweight scrip of unbleached linen, with stout leather straps for the owner's belt. 'I found it dropped between the two beds they had, drawn close together. I don't know which of them owned this one, the two they carried were much alike. But one of them doesn't expect or want ever to come back, does he? Perhaps Matthew does, and has forgotten this, whether he meant it or no, as a pledge.'

Cadfael stared and wondered, but this was a heavy matter, and not for him. He said seriously: 'I think you should bring this with you, and give it into the keeping of Father Abbot. For he sent me to bring you to him. He wants to speak with you.'

'With me?' wavered Rhun, stricken into a wild and rustic child again. 'The lord abbot himself?'

'Surely, and why not? You are Christian soul as he is, and may speak with him as equal.'

The boy faltered: 'I should be afraid . . .'

'No, you would not. You are not afraid of anything, nor need you ever be.'

Rhun sat for a moment with fists doubled into the blanket of his bed; then he lifted his clear, ice-blue gaze and blanched, angelic face and smiled blindingly into Cadfael's eyes. 'No, I need not. I'll come.' And he hoisted the linen scrip and stood up stately on his two long, youthful legs, and led the way to the door.

*   *   *

'Stay with us,' said Abbot Radulfus, when Cadfael would have presented his charge and left the two of them together. 'I think he might be glad of you.' Also, said his eloquent, austere glance, your presence may be of value to me as witness. 'Rhun knows you. Me he does not yet know, but I trust he shall, hereafter.' He had the drab, brownish scrip on the desk before him, offered on entry with a word to account for it, until the time came to explore its possibilities further.

'Willingly, Father,' said Cadfael heartily, and took his seat apart on a stool withdrawn into a corner, out of the way of those two pairs of formidable eyes that met, and wondered, and probed with equal intensity across the small space of the parlour. Outside the windows the garden blossomed with drunken exuberance, in the burning colours of summer,

199

and the blanched blue sky, at its loftiest in the late afternoon, showed the colour of Rhun's eyes, but without their crystal blaze. The day of wonders was drawing very slowly and radiantly towards its evening.

'Son,' said Radulfus at his gentlest, 'you have been the vessel for a great mercy poured out here. I know, as all know who were there, what we saw, what we felt. But I would know also what you passed through. I know you have lived long with pain, and have not complained. I dare guess in what mind you approached the saint's altar. Tell me, what was it happened to you then?'

Rhun sat with his empty hands clasped quietly in his lap, and his face at once remote and easy, looking beyond the walls of the room. All his timidity was lost.

'I was troubled,' he said carefully, 'because my sister and my Aunt Alice wanted so much for me, and I knew I needed nothing. I would have come, and prayed, and passed, and been content. But then I heard her call.'

'Saint Winifred spoke to you?' asked Radulfus softly.

'She called me to her,' said Rhun positively.

'In what words?'

'No words. What need had she of words? She called me to go to her, and I went. She told me, here is a step, and here, and here, come, you know you can. And I knew I could, so I went. When she told me, kneel, for so you

200

can, then I kneeled, and I could. Whatever she told me, that I did. And so I will still,' said Rhun, smiling into the opposing wall with eyes that paled the sun.

'Child,' said the abbot, watching him in solemn wonder and respect, 'I do believe it. What skills you have, what gifts to stead you in your future life, I scarcely know. I rejoice that you have to the full the blessing of your body, and the purity of your mind and spirit. I wish you whatever calling you may choose, and the virtue of your resolve to guide you in it. If there is anything you can ask of this house, to aid you after you go forth from here, it is yours.'

'Father,' said Rhun earnestly, withdrawing his blinding gaze into shadow and mortality, and becoming the child he was, 'need I go forth? She called me to her, how tenderly I have no words to tell. I desire to remain with her to my life's end. She called me to her, and I will never willingly leave her.'

CHAPTER TWELVE

'And will you keep him?' asked Cadfael, when the boy had been dismissed, made his deep reverence, and departed in his rapt, unwitting perfection.

'If his intent holds, yes, surely. He is the living proof of grace. But I will not let him take

201

vows in haste, to regret them later. Now he is transported with joy and wonder, and would embrace celibacy and seclusion with delight. If his will is still the same in a month, then I will believe in it, and welcome him gladly. But he shall serve his full novitiate, even so. I will not let him close the door upon himself until he is sure. And now,' said the abbot, frowning down thoughtfully at the linen scrip that lay upon his desk, 'what is to be done with this? You say it was fallen between the two beds, and might have belonged to either?'

'So the boy said. But, Father, if you remember, when the bishop's ring was stolen, both those young men gave up their scrips to be examined. What each of them carried, apart from the dagger that was duly delivered over at the gatehouse, I cannot say with certainty, but Father Prior, who handled them, will know.'

'True, so he will. But for the present,' said Radulfus, 'I cannot think we have any right to probe into either man's possessions, nor is it of any great importance to discover to which of them this belongs. If Messire de Bretagne overtakes them, as he surely must, we shall learn more, he may even persuade them to return. We'll wait for his word first. In the meantime, leave it here with me. When we know more we'll take whatever steps we can to restore it.'

The day of wonders drew in to its evening as

graciously as it had dawned, with a clear sky and soft, sweet air. Every soul within the enclave came dutifully to Vespers, and supper in the guest-hall as in the refectory was a devout and tranquil feast. The voices hasty and shrill with excitement at dinner had softened and eased into the grateful languor of fulfilment.

Brother Cadfael absented himself from Collations in the chapter house, and went out into the garden. On the gentle ridge where the gradual slope of the pease-fields began he stood for a long while watching the sky. The declining sun had still an hour or more of its course to run before its rim dipped into the feathery tops of the copses across the brook. The west which had reflected the dawn as this day began triumphed now in pale gold, with no wisp of cloud to dye it deeper or mark its purity. The scent of the herbs within the walled garden rose in a heady cloud of sweetness and spice. A good place, a resplendent day—why should any man slip away and run from it?

A useless question. Why should any man do the things he does? Why should Ciaran submit himself to such hardship? Why should he profess such piety and devotion, and yet depart without leave-taking and without thanks in the middle of so auspicious a day? It was Matthew who had left a gift of money on departure. Why could not Matthew persuade his friend to stay and see out the day? And why should he, who had glowed with excited joy in the morning, and run hand in hand with Melangell, abandon her without remorse in the afternoon, and resume his harsh pilgrimage with Ciaran as if nothing had happened?

Were they two men or three? Ciaran, Matthew and Luc Meverel? What did he know of them, all three, if three they were? Luc Meverel had been seen for the last time south of Newbury, walking north towards that town, and alone. Ciaran and Matthew were first reported, by Brother Adam of Reading, coming from the south into Abingdon for their night's lodging, two together. If one of them was Luc Meverel, then where and why had he picked up his companion, and above all, *who was his companion*?

By this time, surely Olivier should have overhauled his quarry, and found the answers to some of these questions. And he had said he would return, that he would not leave Shrewsbury without having some converse with a man remembered as a good friend. Cadfael took that assurance to his heart, and was warmed.

It was not the need to tend any of his herbal potions or bubbling wines that drew him to walk on to his workshop, for Brother Oswin, now in the chapter house with his fellows, had tidied everything for the night, and seen the brazier safely out. There was flint and tinder there in a box, in case it should be necessary to light it again in the night or early in the morning. It was rather that Cadfael had grown accustomed to withdrawing to his own special solitude to do his best thinking, and this day had given him more than enough cause for thought, as for gratitude. For where were his qualms now? Miracles may be spent as frequently on the undeserving as on the deserving. What marvel that a saint should take the boy Rhun to her heart, and reach out her sustaining hand to him? But the second miracle was doubly miraculous, far beyond her sorry servant's asking, stunning in its generosity. To bring him back Olivier, whom he had resigned to God and the great world, and made himself content never to see again! And then Hugh's voice, unwitting herald of wonders, said out of the dim choir, 'And are you demanding yet a second miracle?' He had rather been humbling himself in wonder and thanks for one, demanding nothing more; but he had turned his head, and beheld Olivier.

The western sky was still limpid and bright, liquid gold, the sun still clear of the treetops, when he opened the door of his workshop and stepped within, into the timber-warm, herb-scented dimness. He thought and said afterwards that it was at that moment he saw the inseparable relationship between Ciaran and Matthew suddenly overturned, twisted into its opposite, and began, in some enclosed and detached part of his intelligence, to make sense of the whole matter, however dubious and flawed the revelation. But he had no time to catch and pin down the vision, for as his foot crossed the threshold there was a soft gasp somewhere in the shadowy corner of the hut, and a rustle of movement, as if some wild creature had been disturbed in its lair, and shrunk into the last fastness to defend itself.

He halted, and set the door wide open behind him for reassurance that there was a possibility of escape. 'Be easy!' he said mildly. 'May I not come into my own workshop without leave? And should I be entering here to threaten any soul with harm?'

His eyes, growing accustomed rapidly to the dimness, which seemed dark only by contrast with the radiance outside, scanned the shelves, the bubbling jars of wine in a fat row, the swinging, rustling swathes of herbs dangling from the beams of the low roof. Everything took shape and emerged into view. Stretched along the broad wooden bench against the opposite wall, a huddle of tumbled skirts stirred slowly and reared itself upright, to show him the spilled ripe-corn gold of a girl's hair, and the tear-stained, swollen-lidded countenance of Melangell.

She said no word, but she did not drop blindly into her sheltering arms again. She was long past that, and past being afraid to show herself so to one secret, quiet creature whom

206

she trusted. She set down her feet in their scuffed leather shoes to the floor, and sat back against the timbers of the wall, bracing slight shoulders to the solid contact. She heaved one enormous, draining sigh that was dragged up from her very heels, and left her weak and docile. When he crossed the beaten earth floor and sat down beside her, she did not flinch away.

'Now,' said Cadfael, settling himself with deliberation, to give her time to compose at least her voice. The soft light would spare her face. 'Now, child dear, there is no one here who can either save you or trouble you, and therefore you can speak freely, for everything you say is between us two only. But we two together need to take careful counsel. So what is it you know that I do not know?'

'Why should we take counsel?' she said in a small, drear voice from below his solid shoulder. 'He is gone.'

'What is gone may return. The roads lead always two ways, hither as well as yonder. What are you doing out here alone, when your brother walks erect on two sound feet, and has all he wants in this world, but for your absence?'

He did not look directly at her, but felt the stir of warmth and softness through her body, which must have been a smile, however flawed. 'I came away,' she said, very low, 'not to spoil his joy. I've borne most of the day. I think no one has noticed half my heart was gone out of me. Unless it was you,' she said, without blame, rather in resignation.

'I saw you when we came from Saint Giles,' said Cadfael, 'you and Matthew. Your heart was whole then, so was his. If yours is torn in two now, do you suppose his is preserved without wound? No! So what passed, afterwards? What was this sword that shore through your heart and his? You know! You may tell it now. They are gone, there is nothing left to spoil. There may yet be something to save.'

She turned her forehead into his shoulder and wept in silence for a little while. The light within the hut grew rather than dimming, now that his eyes were accustomed. She forgot to hide her forlorn and bloated face, he saw the bruise on her cheek darkening into purple. He laid an arm about her and drew her close for the comfort of the flesh. That of the spirit would need more of time and thought.

'He struck you?'

'I held him,' she said, quick in his defence. 'He could not get free.'

'And he was so frantic? He *must* go?'

'Yes, whatever it cost him or me. Oh, Brother Cadfael, why? I thought, I believed he loved me, as I do him. But see how he used me in his anger!'

'Anger?' said Cadfael sharply, and turned her by the shoulders to study her more intently. 'Whatever the compulsion on him to go with his friend, why should he be angry with you? The loss was yours, but surely no blame.'

'He blamed me for not telling him,' she said drearily. 'But I did only what Ciaran asked of me. For his sake and yours, he said, yes, and for mine, too, let me go, but hold him fast. Don't tell him I have the ring again, he said, and I will go. Forget me, he said, and help him to forget me. He wanted us to remain together and be happy . . .'

'Are you telling me,' demanded Cadfael sharply, 'that *they did not go together*? That Ciaran made off without him?'

'It was not like that,' sighed Melangell. 'He meant well by us, that's why he stole away alone . . .'

'When was this? When? When did you have speech with him? *When* did he go?'

'I was here at dawn, you'll remember. I met Ciaran by the brook . . .' She drew a deep, desolate breath and loosed the whole flood of it, every word she could recall of that meeting in the early morning, while Cadfael gazed appalled, and the vague glimpse he had had of enlightenment awoke and stirred again in his mind, far clearer now.

'Go on! Tell me what followed between you and Matthew. You did as you were bidden, I know, you drew him with you, I doubt he ever gave a thought to Ciaran all those morning hours, believing him still penned within doors,

209

afraid to stir. When was it he found out?'

'After dinner it came into his mind that he had not seen him. He was very uneasy. He went to look for him everywhere ... He came to me here in the garden. "God keep you, Melangell," he said, "you must fend for yourself now, sorry as I am ..." ' Almost every word of that encounter she had by heart, she repeated them like a tired child repeating a lesson. 'I said too much, he knew I had spoken with Ciaran ... he knew that I knew he'd meant to go secretly ...'

'And then, after you had owned as much?'

'He laughed,' she said, and her very voice froze into a despairing whisper. 'I never heard him laugh until this morning, and then it was such a sweet sound. But this laughter was not so! Bitter and raging.' She stumbled through the rest of it, every word another fine line added to the reversed image that grew in Cadfael's mind, mocking his memory. 'He sets *me* free!' And '*You* must be his confederate!' The words were so burned on her mind that she even reproduced the savagery of their utterance. And how few words it took, in the end, to transform everything, to turn devoted attendance into remorseless pursuit, selfless love into dedicated hatred, noble self-sacrifice into calculated flight, and the voluntary mortification of the flesh into body armour which must never be doffed.

He heard again, abruptly and piercingly,

Ciaran's wild cry of alarm as he clutched his cross to him, and Matthew's voice saying softly: 'Yet he should doff it. How else can he truly be rid of his pains?'

How else, indeed! Cadfael recalled, too, how he had reminded them both that they were here to attend the feast of a saint who might have life itself within her gift—'even for a man already condemned to death!' Oh, Saint Winifred, stand by me now, stand by us all, with a third miracle to better the other two!

He took Melangell brusquely by the chin, and lifted her face to him. 'Girl, look to yourself now for a while, for I must leave you. Do up your hair and keep a brave face, and go back to your kin as soon as you can bear their eyes on you. Go into the church for a time, it will be quiet there now, and who will wonder if you give a longer time to your prayers? They will not even wonder at past tears, if you can smile now. Do as well as you can, for I have a thing I must do.'

There was nothing he could promise her, no sure hope he could leave with her. He turned from her without another word, leaving her staring after him between dread and reassurance, and went striding in haste through the gardens and out across the court, to the abbot's lodging.

* * *

If Radulfus was surprised to have Cadfael ask audience again so soon, he gave no sign of it, but had him admitted at once, and put aside his book to give his full attention to whatever this fresh business might be. Plainly it was something very much to the current purpose and urgent.

'Father,' said Cadfael, making short work of explanations, 'there's a new twist here. Messire de Bretagne has gone off on a false trail. Those two young men did not leave by the Oswestry road, but crossed the Meole brook and set off due west to reach Wales the nearest way. Nor did they leave together. Ciaran slipped away during the morning, while his fellow was with us in the procession, and Matthew has followed him by the same way as soon as he learned of his going. And, Father, there's good cause to think that the sooner they're overtaken and halted, the better surely for one, and I believe for both. I beg you, let me take a horse and follow. And send word of this to Hugh Beringar in the town, to come after us on the same trail.'

Radulfus received all this with a grave but calm face, and asked no less shortly: 'How did you come by this word?'

'From the girl who spoke with Ciaran before he departed. No need to doubt it is all true. And, Father, one more thing before you bid me go. Open, I beg you, that scrip they left behind, let me see if it has anything more to tell us of this pair—at the least, of one of them.'

Without a word or an instant of hesitation, Radulfus dragged the linen scrip into the light of his candles, and unbuckled the fastening. The contents he drew out fully upon the desk, sparse enough, what the poor pilgrim would carry, having few possessions and desiring to travel light.

'You know, I think,' said the abbot, looking up sharply, 'to which of the two this belonged?'

'I do not know, but I guess. In my mind I am sure, but I am also fallible. Give me leave!'

With a sweep of his hand he spread the meagre belongings over the desk. The purse, thin enough when Prior Robert had handled it before, lay flat and empty now. The leather-bound breviary, well-used, worn but treasured, had been rolled into the folds of the shirt, and when Cadfael reached for it the shirt slid from the desk and fell to the floor. He let it lie as he opened the book. Within the cover was written, in a clerk's careful hand, the name of its owner: 'Juliana Bossard.' And below, in newer ink and a less practised hand: *Given to me, Luc Meverel, this Christmastide, 1140. God be with us all!*

'So I pray, too,' said Cadfael, and stooped to pick up the fallen shirt. He held it up to the light, and his eye caught the thread-like outline of a stain that rimmed the left shoulder. His eye followed the line over the

213

shoulder, and found it continued down and round the left side of the breast. The linen, otherwise, was clean enough, bleached by several launderings from its original brownish natural colouring. He spread it open, breast up, on the desk. The thin brown line, sharp on its outer edge, slightly blurred within, hemmed a great space spanning the whole left part of the chest and the upper part of the left sleeve. The space within the outline had been washed clear of any stain, even the rim was pale, but it stood clear to be seen, and the scattered shadowings of colour within it preserved a faint hint of what had been there.

Radulfus, if he had not ventured as far afield in the world as Cadfael, had nevertheless stored up some experience of it. He viewed the extended evidence and said composedly, 'This was blood.'

'So it was,' said Cadfael, and rolled up the shirt.

'And whoever owned this scrip came from where a certain Juliana Bossard was chatelaine.' His deep eyes were steady and sombre on Cadfael's face. 'Have we entertained a murderer in our house?'

'I think we have,' said Cadfael, restoring the scattered fragments of a life to their modest lodging. A man's life, shorn of all expectation of continuance, even the last coin gone from the purse. 'But I think we may have time yet to prevent another killing—if you give me leave to go.'

'Take the best of what may be in the stable,' said the abbot simply, 'and I will send word to Hugh Beringar, and have him follow you, and not alone.'

CHAPTER THIRTEEN

Several miles north on the Oswestry road, Olivier drew rein by the roadside where a wiry, bright-eyed boy was grazing goats on the broad verge, lush in summer growth and coming into seed. The child twitched one of his long leads on his charges, to bring him along gently where the early evening light lay warm on the tall grass. He looked up at the rider without awe, half-Welsh and immune from servility. He smiled and gave an easy good evening.

The boy was handsome, bold, unafraid; so was the man. They looked at each other and liked what they saw.

'God be with you!' said Olivier. 'How long have you been pasturing your beasts along here? And have you in all that time seen a lame man and a well man go by, the pair of them much of my age, but afoot?'

'God be with you, master,' said the boy cheerfully. 'Here along this verge ever since noon, for I brought my bit of dinner with me. But I've seen none such pass. And I've had a word by the road with every soul that did go by, unless he were galloping.'

'Then I waste my hurrying,' said Olivier, and idled a while, his horse stooping to the tips of the grasses. 'They cannot be ahead of me, not by this road. See, now, supposing they wished to go earlier into Wales, how may I bear round to pick them up on the way? They went from Shrewsbury town ahead of me, and I have word to bring to them. Where can I turn west and fetch a circle about the town?'

The young herdsman accepted with open arms every exchange that refreshed his day's labour. He gave his mind to the best road offering, and delivered judgement: 'Turn back but a mile or more, back across the bridge at Montford, and then you'll find a well-used cart-track that bears off west, to your right hand it will be. Bear a piece west again where the paths first branch, it's no direct way, but it does go on. It skirts Shrewsbury a matter of above four miles outside the town, and threads the edges of the forest, but it cuts across every path out of Shrewsbury. You may catch your men yet. And I wish you may!'

'My thanks for that,' said Olivier, 'and for your advice also.' He stooped to the hand the boy had raised, not for alms but to caress the horse's chestnut shoulder with admiration and pleasure, and slipped a coin into the smooth palm. 'God be with you!' he said, and wheeled his mount and set off back along the road he had travelled.

'And go with you, master!' the boy called after him, and watched until a curve of the road took horse and rider out of sight beyond a stand of trees. The goats gathered closer; evening was near, and they were ready to turn homeward, knowing the hour by the sun as well as did their herd. The boy drew in their tethers, whistled to them cheerily, and moved on along the road to his homeward path through the fields.

Olivier came for the second time to the bridge over the Severn, one bank a steep, tree-clad escarpment, the other open, level meadow. Beyond the first plane of fields a winding track turned off to the right, between scattered stands of trees, bearing at this point rather south than west, but after a mile or more it brought him on to a better road that crossed his track left and right. He bore right into the sun, as he had been instructed, and at the next place where two dwindling paths divided he turned left, and keeping his course by the sinking sun on his right hand, now just resting upon the rim of the world and glimmering through the trees in sudden blinding glimpses, began to work his way gradually round the town of Shrewsbury. The tracks wound in and out of copses, the fringe woods of the northern tip of the Long Forest, sometimes in twilight among dense trees, sometimes in open heath and scrub, sometimes past islets of cultivated fields and glimpses of hamlets. He rode with ears pricked for any promising sound, pausing wherever his labyrinthine path crossed a track bearing westward out of Shrewsbury, and wherever he met with cottage or assart he asked after his two travellers. No one had seen such a pair pass by. Olivier took heart. They had had some hours start of him, but if they had not passed westward by any of the roads he had yet crossed, they might still be within the circle he was drawing about the town. The barefoot one would not find these ways easy going, and might have been forced to take frequent rests. At the worst, even if he missed them in the end, this meandering route must bring him round at last to the highroad by which he had first approached Shrewsbury from the southeast, and he could ride back into the town to Hugh Beringar's welcome, none the worse for a little exercise in a fine evening.

*   *   *

Brother Cadfael had wasted no time in clambering into his boots, kilting his habit, and taking and saddling the best horse he could find in the stables. It was not often he had the chance to indulge himself with such half-forgotten delights, but he was not thinking of that now. He had left considered word with the messenger who was already hurrying across the bridge and into the town, to alert Hugh; and Hugh would ask no questions, as the abbot had asked none, recognising the grim urgency there was no leisure now to explain.

'Say to Hugh Beringar,' the order ran, 'that Ciaran will make for the Welsh border the nearest way, but avoiding the too open roads. I think he'll bear south a small way to the old road the Romans made, that we've been fools enough to let run wild, for it keeps a steady level and makes straight for the border north of Caus.'

That was drawing a bow at a venture, and he knew it, none better. Ciaran was not of these parts, though he might well have some knowledge of the borderland if he had kin on the Welsh side. But more than that, he had been here these three days past, and if he had been planning some such escape all that time, he could have picked the brains of brothers and guests, on easily plausible ground. Time pressed, and sound guessing was needed. Cadfael chose his way, and set about pursuing it.

He did not waste time in going decorously out at the gatehouse and round by the road to take up the chase westward, but led his horse at a trot through the gardens, to the blank astonishment of Brother Jerome, who happened to be crossing to the cloisters a good ten minutes early for Compline. No doubt he would report, with a sense of outrage, to Prior Robert. Cadfael as promptly forgot him, leading the horse round the unharvested pease-field and down to the quiet green stretches of the brook, and across to the narrow meadow, where he mounted. The sun was dipping its rim beyond the crowns of the trees to westward. Into that half-shine, half-shadow Cadfael spurred, and made good speed while the tracks were familiar to him as his own palm. Due west until he hit the road, a half-mile on the road at a canter, until it turned too far to the south, and then westward again for the setting sun. Ciaran had a long start, even of Matthew, let alone of all those who followed now. But Ciaran was lame, burdened and afraid. Almost he was to be pitied.

Half a mile further on, at an inconspicuous track which he knew, Cadfael again turned to bear south-west, and burrowed into deepest shade, and into the northernmost woodlands of the Long Forest. No more than a narrow forest ride, this, between sweeping branches, a fragment of ancient wood not worth clearing for an assart, being bedded on rock that broke surface here and there. This was not yet border country, but close kin to it, heaving into fretful outcrops that broke the thin soil, bearing heather and coarse upland grasses, scrub bushes and sparsity trees, then bringing forth prodigal life roofed by very old trees in every wet hollow. A little further on this course, and the close, dark woods began, tall top cover, heavy interweaving of middle growth, and a tangle of bush and bramble and ground-cover below. Undisturbed forest, though there were rare islands of tillage bright and open within it, every one an astonishment.

Then he came to the old, old road, that sliced like a knife across his path, heading due east, due west. He wondered about the men who had made it. It was shrunken now from a soldiers' road to a narrow ride, mostly under thin turf, but it ran as it had always run since it was made, true and straight as a lance, perfectly levelled where a level was possible, relentlessly climbing and descending where some hummock barred the way. Cadfael turned west into it, and rode straight for the golden upper arc of sun that still glowed between the branches.

*   *   *

In the parcel of old forest north and west of the hamlet of Hanwood there were groves where stray outlaws could find ample cover, provided they stayed clear of the few settlements within reach. Local people tended to fence their holdings and band together to protect their own small ground. The forest was for plundering, poaching, pasturing of swine, all with secure precautions. Travellers, though they might call on hospitality and aid where needed, must fend for themselves in the thicker coverts, if they cared to venture through them. By and large, safety here in Shropshire under Hugh Beringar was as good as anywhere in England, and encroachment by vagabonds could not survive long, but for brief occupation the cover was there, and unwanted tenants might take up occupation if pressed.

Several of the lesser manors in these border regions had declined by reason of their perilous location, and some were half-deserted, leaving their fields untilled. Until April of this year the border castle of Caus had been in Welsh hands, an added threat to peaceful occupation, and there had not yet been time since Hugh's reclamation of the castle for the depleted hamlets to re-establish themselves. Moreover, in this high summer it was no hardship to live wild, and skilful poaching and a little profitable thievery could keep two or three good fellows in meat while they allowed time for their exploits in the south to be forgotten, and made up their minds where best to pass the time until a return home seemed possible.

Master Simeon Poer, self-styled merchant of Guildford, was not at all ill-content with the pickings made in Shrewsbury. In three nights, which was the longest they dared reckon on operating unsuspected, they had taken a fair amount of money from the hopeful gamblers of the town and Foregate, besides the price Daniel Aurifaber had paid for the stolen ring, the various odds and ends William Hales had abstracted from market stalls, and the coins John Shure had used his long, smooth, waxed finger-nails to extract from pocket and purse in the crowds. It was a pity they had had to leave William Hales to his fate during the raid, but all in all they had done well to get out of it with no more than a bruise or two, and one man short. Bad luck for William, but it was the way the lot had fallen. Every man knew it could happen to him.

They had avoided the used tracks, refraining from meddling with any of the local people going about their business, and done their plundering by night and stealthily, after first making sure where there were dogs to be reckoned with. They even had a roof of sorts, for in the deepest thickets below the old road, overgrown and well-concealed, they had found the remains of a hut, relic of a failed assart abandoned long ago. After a few days more of this easy living, or if the weather should change, they would set off to make their way somewhat south, to be well clear of Shrewsbury before moving across to the east, to shires where they were not yet known.

When the rare traveller came past on the road, it was almost always a local man, and they let him alone, for he would be missed all too soon, and the hunt would be up in a day.

But they would not have been averse to waylaying any solitary who was clearly a stranger and on his way to more distant places, since he was unlikely to be missed at once, and further, he was likely to be better worth robbing, having on him the means to finance his journey, however modestly. In these woods and thickets, a man could vanish very neatly, and for ever.

They had made themselves comfortable that night outside their hut, with the embers of their fire safe in the clay-lined hollow they had made for it, and the grease of the stolen chicken still on their fingers. The sunset of the outer world was already twilight here, but they had their night eyes, and were wide awake and full of restless energy after an idle day. Walter Bagot was charged with keeping such watch as they thought needful, and had made his way in cover some distance along the narrow track towards the town. He came sliding back in haste, but shining with anticipation instead of alarm.

'Here's one coming we may safely pick off. The barefoot fellow from the abbey ... well back as yet, and lame as ever, he's been among the stones, surely. Not a soul will know where he went to.'

'He?' said Simeon Poer, surprised. 'Fool, he has always his shadow breathing down his neck. It would mean both—if one got away he'd raise the hunt on us.'

'He has not his shadow now,' said Bagot gleefully. 'Alone, I tell you, he's shaken him off, or else they've parted by consent. Who else cares a groat what becomes of him?'

'And a groat's his worth,' said Shure scornfully. 'Let him go. It's never worth it for his hose and shirt, and what else can he have on him?'

'Ah, but he has! Money, my friend!' said Bagot, glittering. 'Make no mistake, that one goes very well provided, if he takes good care not to let it be known. I know! I've felt my way about him every time I could get crowded against him in church, he has a solid, heavy purse belted about him inside coat, hose, shirt and all, but I never could get my fingers into it without using the knife, and that was too risky. He can pay his way wherever he goes. Come, rouse, he'll be an easy mark now.'

He was certain, and they were heartily willing to pick up an extra purse. They rose merrily, hands on daggers, worming their way quietly through the underbrush towards the thin thread of the track, above which the ribbon of clear sky showed pale and bright still. Shure and Bagot lurking invisible on the near side of the path, Simeon Poer across it, behind the lush screen of bushes that took advantage of the open light to grow leafy and tall. There were very old trees in their tract of forest, enormous beeches with trunks so gnarled and thick three men with arms

225

outspread could hardly clip them. Old woodland was being cleared, assarted and turned into hunting-grounds in many places, but the Long Forest still preserved large tracts of virgin growth untouched. In the green dimness the three masterless men stood still as the trees, and waited.

Then they heard him. Dogged, steady, laborious steps that stirred the coarse grasses. In the turfed verge of a highroad he could have gone with less pain and covered twice the miles he had accomplished on these rough ways. They heard his heavy breathing while he was still twenty yards away from them, and saw his tall, dark figure stir the dimness, leaning forward on a long, knotty staff he had picked up somewhere from among the debris of the trees. It seemed that he favoured the right foot, though both trod with wincing tenderness, as though he had trodden askew on a sharp-edged stone, and either cut his sole or twisted his ankle-joint. He was piteous, if there had been anyone to pity him.

He went with ears pricked, and the very hairs of his skin erected, in as intense wariness as any of the small nocturnal creatures that crept and quaked in the underbrush around him. He had walked in fear every step of the miles he had gone in company, but now, cast loose to his own dreadful company, he was even more afraid. Escape was no escape at all.

It was the extremity of his fear that saved

him. They had let him pass slowly by the first covert, so that Bagot might be behind him, and Poer and Shure one on either side before him. It was not so much his straining ears as the prickly sensitivity of his skin that sensed the sudden rushing presence at his back, the shifting of the cool evening air, and the weight of body and arm launched at him almost silently. He gave a muted shriek and whirled about, sweeping the staff around him, and the knife that should have impaled him struck the branch and sliced a ribbon of bark and wood from it. Bagot reached with his left hand for a grip on sleeve or coat, and struck again as nimbly as a snake, but missed his hold as Ciaran leaped wildly back out of reach, and driven beyond himself by terror, turned and plunged away on his lacerated feet, aside from the path and into the deepest and thickest shadows among the tangled trees. He hissed and moaned with pain as he went, but he ran like a startled hare.

Who would have thought he could still move so fast, once pushed to extremes? But he could not keep it up long, the spur would not carry him far. The three of them went after, spreading out a little to hem him from three sides when he fell exhausted. They were giggling as they went, and in no special haste. The mingled sounds of his crashing passage through the bushes and his uncontrollable whining with the pain of it, rang unbelievably strangely in the twilit woods.

Branches and brambles lashed Ciaran's face. He ran blindly, sweeping the long staff before him, cutting a noisy swathe through the bushes and stumbling painfully in the thick ground-debris of dead branches and soft, treacherous pits of the leaves of many years. They followed at leisure, aware that he was slowing. The lean, agile tailor had drawn level with him, somewhat aside, and was bearing round to cut him off, still with breath enough to whistle to his fellows as they closed unhurriedly, like dogs herding a stray sheep. Ciaran fell out into a more open glade, where a huge old beech had preserved its own clearing, and with what was left of his failing breath he made a last dash to cross the open and vanish again into the thickets beyond. The dry silt of leaves among the roots betrayed him. His footing slid from under him, and fetched him down heavily against the bole of the tree. He had just time to drag himself up and set his back to the broad trunk before they were on him.

He flailed about him with the staff, screaming for aid, and never even knew on what name he was calling in his extremity.

'Help! Murder! Matthew, Matthew, help me!'

There was no answering shout, but there was an abrupt thrashing of branches, and something hurtled out of cover and across the grass, so suddenly that Bagot was shouldered aside and stumbled to his knees. A long arm swept Ciaran back hard against the solid bole of the tree, and Matthew stood braced beside him, his dagger naked in his hand. What remained of the western light showed his face roused and formidable, and gleamed along the blade.

'Oh, no!' he challenged loud and clear, lips drawn back from bared teeth. 'Keep your hands off! This man is mine!'

CHAPTER FOURTEEN

The three attackers had drawn off instinctively, before they realised that this was but one man erupting in their midst, but they were quick to grasp it, and had not gone far. They stood, wary as beasts of prey but undeterred, weaving a little in a slow circle out of reach, but with no thought of withdrawing. They watched and considered, weighing up coldly these altered odds. Two men and a knife to reckon with now, and this second one they knew as well as the first. They had been some days frequenting the same enclave, using the same dortoir and refectory. They reasoned without dismay that they must be known as well as they knew their prey. The twilight made faces shadowy, but a man is recognised by more things than his face.

'I said it, did I not?' said Simeon Poer, exchanging glances with his henchmen, glances which were understood even in the dim light. 'I said he would not be far. No matter, two can lie as snug as one.'

Once having declared his claim and his rights, Matthew said nothing. The tree against which they braced themselves was so grown that they could not be attacked from close behind. He circled it steadily when Bagot edged round to the far side, keeping his face to the enemy. There were three to watch, and Ciaran was shaken and lame, and in no case to match any of the three if it came to action, though he kept his side of the trunk with his staff gripped and ready, and would fight if he must, tooth and claw, for his forfeit life. Matthew curled his lips in a bitter smile at the thought that he might be grateful yet for that strong appetite for living.

Round the bole of the tree, with his cheek against the bark, Ciaran said, low-voiced: 'You'd have done better not to follow me.'

'Did I not swear to go with you to the very end?' said Matthew as softly. 'I keep my vows. This one above all.'

'Yet you could still have crept away safely. Now we are two dead men.'

'Not yet! If you did not want me, why did you call me?'

There was a bewildered silence. Ciaran did

not know he had uttered a name.

'We are grown used to each other,' said Matthew grimly. 'You claimed me, as I claim you. Do you think I'll let any other man have you?'

The three watchers had gathered in a shadowy group, conferring with heads together, and faces still turned towards their prey.

'Now they'll come,' said Ciaran in the dead voice of despair.

'No, they'll wait for darkness.'

They were in no hurry. They made no loose, threatening moves, wasted no breath on words. They bided their time as patiently as hunting animals. Silently they separated, spacing themselves round the clearing, and backing just far enough into cover to be barely visible, yet visible all the same, for their presence and stillness were meant to unnerve. Just so, motionless, relentless and alert, would a cat sit for hours outside a mousehole.

'This I cannot bear,' said Ciaran in a faint whisper, and drew sobbing breath.

'It is easily cured,' said Matthew through his teeth. 'You have only to lift off that cross from your neck, and you can be loosed from all your troubles.'

The light faded still. Their eyes, raking the smoky darkness of the bushes, were beginning to see movement where there was none, and strain in vain after it where it lurked and shifted to baffle them more. This waiting would not be long. The attackers circled in cover, watching for the unguarded moment when one or other of their victims would be caught unawares, staring in the wrong direction. Past all question they would expect that failure first from Ciaran, half-foundering as he already was. Soon now, very soon.

*   *   *

Brother Cadfael was some half-mile back along the ride when he heard the cry, ahead and to the right of the path, loud, wild and desperate. The words were indistinguishable, but the panic in the sound there was no mistaking. In this woodland silence, without even a wind to stir the branches or flutter the leaves, every sound carried clearly. Cadfael spurred ahead in haste, with all too dire a conviction of what he might find when he reached the source of that lamentable cry. All those miles of pursuit, patient and remorseless, half the length of England, might well be ending now, barely a quarter of an hour too soon for him to do anything to prevent. Matthew had overtaken, surely, a Ciaran grown weary of his penitential austerities, now there was no one by to see. He had said truly enough that he did not hate himself so much as to bear his hardships to no purpose. Now that he was alone, had he felt

232

safe in discarding his heavy cross, and would he next have been in search of shoes for his feet? If Matthew had not come upon him thus recreant and disarmed.

The second sound to break the stillness almost passed unnoticed because of the sound of his own progress, but he caught some quiver of the forest's unease, and reined in to listen intently. The rush and crash of something or someone hurtling through thick bushes, fast and arrow-straight, and then, very briefly, a confusion of cries, not loud but sharp and wary, and a man's voice loud and commanding over all. Matthew's voice, not in triumph or terror, rather in short and resolute defiance. There were more than the two of them, there ahead, and not so far ahead now.

He dismounted, and led his horse at an anxious trot as far as he dared along the path, towards the spot from which the sounds had come. Hugh could move very fast when he saw reason, and in Cadfael's bare message he would have found reason enough. He would have left the town by the most direct way, over the western bridge and so by a good road south west, to strike this old path barely two miles back. At this moment he might be little more than a mile behind. Cadfael tethered his horse at the side of the track, for a plain sign that he had found cause to halt here and was somewhere close by.

All was quiet about him now. He quested

along the fringe of bushes for a place where he might penetrate without any betraying noise, and began to work his way by instinct and touch towards the place whence the cries had come, and where now all was almost unnaturally silent. In a little while he was aware of the last faint pallor of the afterglow glimmering between the branches. There was a more open glade ahead of him.

He froze and stood motionless, as a shadow passed silently between him and this lingering glimpse of light. Someone tall and lean, slithering snake-like through the bushes. Cadfael waited until the faint pattern of light was restored, and then edged carefully forward until he could see into the clearing.

The great bole of a beech-tree showed in the centre, a solid mass beneath its spread of branches. There was movement there in the dimness. Not one man, but two, stood pressed against the bole. A brief flash of steel caught just light enough to show what it was, a dagger naked and ready. Two at bay here, and surely more than one pinning them thus helpless until they could be safely pulled down. Cadfael stood still to survey the whole of the darkening clearing, and found, as he had expected, another quiver of leaves that hid a man, and then, on the opposite side, yet another. Three, probably all armed, certainly up to no good, thus furtively prowling the woods by night, going nowhere, waiting to make the kill. Three had vanished from the dice school under the bridge at Shrewsbury, and fled in this direction. Three reappeared here in the forest, still doing after their disreputable kind.

Cadfael stood hesitant, pondering how best to deal, whether to steal back to the path and wait and hope for Hugh's coming, or attempt something alone, at least to distract and dismay, to bring about a delay that might afford time for help to come. He had made up his mind to return to his horse, mount, and ride in here with as much noise and turmoil as he could muster, trying to sound like six mounted men instead of one, when with shattering suddenness the decision was taken out of his hands.

One of the three besiegers sprang out of cover with a startling shout, and rushed at the tree on the side where the momentary flash of steel had shown one of the victims, at least, to be armed. A dark figure leaned out from the darkness under the branches to meet the onslaught, and Cadfael knew him then for Matthew. The attacker swerved aside, still out of reach, in a calculated feint, and at the same moment both the other lurking shadows burst out of cover and bore down upon the other side of the tree, falling as one upon the weaker opponent. There was a confusion of violence, and a wild, tormented scream, and Matthew whirled about, slashing round him and stretching a long arm across his companion, pinning him back against the tree. Ciaran hung half-fainting, slipping down between the great, smooth bastions of the bole, and Matthew bestrode him, his dagger sweeping great swathes before them both.

Cadfael saw it, and was held mute and motionless, beholding this devoted enemy. He got his breath only as all three of the predators closed upon their prey together, slashing, mauling, by sheer weight bearing them down under them.

Cadfael filled his lungs full, and bellowed to the shaken night: 'Hold, there! On them, hold them all three. These are our felons!' He was making so much noise that he did not notice or marvel that the echoes, which in his fury he heard but did not heed, came from two directions at once, from the path he had left, and from the opposite point, from the north. Some corner of his mind knew he had roused echoes, but for his part he felt himself quite alone as he kept up his roaring, spread his sleeves like the wings of a bat, and surged headlong into the mêlée about the tree.

Long, long ago he had forsworn arms, but what of it? Barring his two stout fists, still active but somewhat rheumatic now, he was unarmed. He flung himself into the tangle of men and weapons under the beech, laid hands on the back of a dangling capuchon, hauled its wearer bodily backwards, and twisted the cloth to choke the throat that howled rage and venom at him. But his voice had done more than his martial progress. The black huddle of humanity burst into its separate beings. Two sprang clear and looked wildly about them for the source of the alarm, and Cadfael's opponent reached round, gasping, with a long arm and a vicious dagger, and sliced a dangling streamer out of a rusty black sleeve. Cadfael lay on him with all his weight, held him by the hair, and ground his face into the earth, shamelessly exulting. He would do penance for it some day soon, but now he rejoiced, all his crusader blood singing in his veins.

Distantly he was aware that something else was happening, more than he had reckoned on. He heard and felt the unmistakable quiver and thud of the earth reacting to hooves, and heard a peremptory voice shouting orders, the purport of which he did not release his grip to decipher or attend to. The glade was filled with motion as it filled with darkness. The creature under him gathered itself and heaved mightily, rolling him aside. His hold on the folds of the hood relaxed, and Simeon Poer tore himself free and scrambled clear. There was running every way, but none of the fugitives got far.

Last of the three to roll breathless out of hold, Simeon groped about him vengefully in the roots of the tree, touched a cowering body, found the cord of some dangling relic, possibly precious, in his hand, and hauled with all his

237

strength before he gathered himself up and ran for cover. There was a wild scream of pain, and the cord broke, and the thing, whatever it was, came loose in his hand. He got his feet under him, and charged head-down for the nearest bushes, hurtled into them and ran, barely a yard clear of hands that stooped from horse-back to claw at him.

Cadfael opened his eyes and hauled in breath. The whole clearing was boiling with movement, the darkness heaved and trembled, and the violence had ordered itself into purpose and meaning. He sat up, and took his time to look about him. He was sprawled under the great beech, and somewhere before him, towards the path where he had left his horse, someone with flint and dagger and tinder, was striking sparks for a torch, very calmly. The sparks caught, glowed, and were gently blown into flame. The torch, well primed with oil and resin, sucked in the flame and gave birth to a small, shapely flame of its own, that grew and reared, and was used to kindle a second and a third. The clearing took on a small, confined, rounded shape, walled with close growth, roofed with the tree.

Hugh came out of the dark, smiling, and reached a hand to haul him to his feet. Someone else came running light-footed from the other side, and stooped to him a wonderful, torch-lit face, high-boned, lean-cheeked, with eager golden eyes, and blue-black raven wings of hair curving to cup his cheeks.

'Olivier?' said Cadfael, marvelling. 'I thought you were astray on the road to Oswestry. How did you ever find us here?'

'By grace of God and a goat-herd,' said the warm, gay, remembered voice, 'and your bull's bellowing. Come, look round! You have won your field.'

They were gone, Simeon Poer, merchant of Guildford, Walter Bagot, glover, John Shure, tailor, all fled, but with half a dozen of Hugh's men hard on their heels, all to be brought in captive, to answer for more, this time, than a little cheating in the marketplace. Night stooped to enfold a closed arena of torchlight, very quiet now and almost still. Cadfael rose, his torn sleeve dangling awkwardly. The three of them stood in a half-circle about the beech-tree.

The torchlight was stark, plucking light and shadow into sharp relief. Matthew stirred out of his colloquy between life and death very slowly as they watched him, heaved his wide shoulders clear of the tree, and stood forth like a sleeper roused before his time, looking about him as if for something by which he might hold, and take his bearings. Between his feet, as he emerged, the coiled, crumpled form of Ciaran came into view, faintly stirring, his head huddled into his close-folded arms.

'Get up!' said Matthew. He drew back a

239

little from the tree, his naked dagger in his hand, a slow drop gathering at its tip, more drops falling steadily from the hand that held it. His knuckles were sliced raw. 'Get up!' he said. 'You are not harmed.'

Ciaran gathered himself very slowly, and clambered to his knees, lifting to the light a face soiled and leaden, gone beyond exhaustion, beyond fear. He looked neither at Cadfael nor at Hugh, but stared up into Matthew's face with the helpless intensity of despair. Hugh felt the clash of eyes, and stirred to make some decisive movement and break the tension, but Cadfael laid a hand on his arm and held him still. Hugh gave him a sharp sidelong glance, and accepted the caution. Cadfael had his reasons.

There was blood on the torn collar of Ciaran's shirt, a stain that grew sluggishly before their eyes. He put up hands that seemed heavy as lead, and fumbled aside the linen from throat and breast. All round the left side of his neck ran a raw, bleeding slash, thin as a knife-cut. Simeon Poer's last blind clutch for plunder had torn loose the cross to which Ciaran had clung so desperately. He kneeled in the last wretched extreme of submission, baring a throat already symbolically slit.

'Here am I,' he said in a toneless whisper. 'I can run no further, I am forfeit. Now take me!'

Matthew stood motionless, staring at that savage cut the cord had left before it broke.

The silence grew too heavy to be bearable, and still he had no word to say, and his face was a blank mask in the flickering light of the torches.

'He says right,' said Cadfael, very softly and reasonably. 'He is yours fairly. The terms of his penance are broken, and his life is forfeit. Take him!'

There was no sign that Matthew so much as heard him, but for the spasmodic tightening of his lips, as if in pain. He never took his eyes from the wretch kneeling humbly before him.

'You have followed him faithfully, and kept the terms laid down,' Cadfael urged gently. 'You are under vow. Now finish the work!'

He was on safe enough ground, and sure of it now. The act of submission had already finished the work, there was no more to be done. With his enemy at his mercy, and every justification for the act of vengeance, the avenger was helpless, the prisoner of his own nature. There was nothing left in him but a drear sadness, a sick revulsion of disgust and self-disgust. How could he kill a wretched, broken man, kneeling here unresisting, waiting for his death? Death was no longer relevant.

'It is over, Luc,' said Cadfael softly. 'Do what you must.'

Matthew stood mute a moment longer, and if he had heard his true name spoken, he gave no sign, it was of no importance. After the abandonment of all purpose came the awful

241

sense of loss and emptiness. He opened his blood-stained hand and let the dagger slip from his fingers into the grass. He turned away like a blind man, feeling with a stretched foot for every step, groped his way through the curtain of bushes, and vanished into the darkness.

Olivier drew in breath sharply, and started out of his tranced stillness to catch eagerly at Cadfael's arm. 'Is it true? You have found him out? *He* is Luc Meverel?' He accepted the truth of it without another word said, and sprang ardently towards the place where the bushes still stirred after Luc's passing, and he would have been off in pursuit at a run if Hugh had not caught at his arm to detain him.

'Wait but one moment! You also have a cause here, if Cadfael is right. This is surely the man who murdered your friend. He owes you a death. He is yours if you want him.'

'That is truth,' said Cadfael. 'Ask him! He will tell you.'

Ciaran crouched in the grass, drooping now, bewildered and lost, no longer looking any man in the face, only waiting without hope or understanding for someone to determine whether he was to live or die, and on what abject terms. Olivier cast one wondering glance at him, shook his head in emphatic rejection, and reached for his horse's bridle. 'Who am I,' he said, 'to exact what Luc Meverel has remitted? Let this one go on his

242

way with his own burden. My business is with the other.'

He was away at a run, leading the horse briskly through the screen of bushes, and the rustling of their passage gradually stilled again into silence. Cadfael and Hugh were left regarding each other mutely across the lamentable figure crouched upon the ground.

Gradually the rest of the world flowed back into Cadfael's ken. Three of Hugh's officers stood aloof with the horses and the torches, looking on in silence; and somewhere not far distant sounded a brief scuffle and outcry, as one of the fugitives was overpowered and made prisoner. Simeon Poer had been pulled down barely fifty yards in cover, and stood sullenly under guard now, with his wrists secured to a sergeant's stirrup-leather. The third would not be a free man long. This night's ventures were over. This piece of woodland would be safe even for barefoot and unarmed pilgrims to traverse.

'What is to be done with him?' demanded Hugh openly, looking down upon the wreckage of a man with some distaste.

'Since Luc has waived his claim,' said Cadfael, 'I would not dare meddle. And there is something at least to be said for him, he did not cheat or break his terms voluntarily, even when there was no one by to accuse him. It is a small virtue to have to advance for the defence of a life, but it is something. Who else has the right to foreclose on what Luc has spared?'

Ciaran raised his head, peering doubtfully from one face to the other, still confounded at being so spared, but beginning to believe that he still lived. He was weeping, whether with pain, or relief, or something more durable than either, there was no telling. The blood was blackening into a dark line about his throat.

'Speak up and tell truth,' said Hugh with chill gentleness. 'Was it you who stabbed Bossard?'

Out of the pallid disintegration of Ciaran's face a wavering voice said: 'Yes.'

'Why did you so? Why attack the queen's clerk, who did nothing but deliver his errand faithfully?'

Ciaran's eyes burned for an instant, and a fleeting spark of past pride, intolerance and rage showed like the last glow of a dying fire. 'He came high-handed, shouting down the lord bishop, defying the council. My master was angry and affronted . . .'

'Your master,' said Cadfael, 'was the prior of Hyde Mead. Or so you claimed.'

'How could I any longer claim service with one who had discarded me? I lied! The lord bishop himself—I served Bishop Henry, had his favour. Lost, lost now! I could not brook the man Christian's insolence to him . . . he stood against everything my lord planned and willed. I hated him! I thought then that I hated

244

him,' said Ciaran, drearily wondering at the recollection. 'And I thought to please my lord!'

'A calculation that went awry,' said Cadfael, 'for whatever he may be, Henry of Blois is no murderer. And Rainald Bossard prevented your mischief, a man of your own party, held in esteem. Did that make him a traitor in your eyes—that he should respect an honest opponent? Or did you strike out at random, and kill without intent?'

'No,' said the level, lame voice, bereft of its brief spark. 'He thwarted me, I was enraged. I knew what I did. I was glad . . . *then*!' he said, and drew bitter breath.

'And who laid upon you this penitential journey?' asked Cadfael, 'and to what end? Your life was granted you, upon terms. What terms? Someone in the highest authority laid that load upon you.'

'My lord the bishop-legate,' said Ciaran, and wrung wordlessly for a moment at the pain of an old devotion, rejected and banished now for ever. 'There was no other soul knew of it, only to him I told it. He would not give me up to law, he wanted this thing put by, for fear it should threaten his plans for the empress's peace. But he would not condone. I am from the Danish kingdom of Dublin, my other half Welsh. He offered me passage under his protection to Bangor, to the bishop there, who would see me to Caergybi in Anglesey, and have me put aboard a ship for Dublin. But I must go barefoot all that way, and wear the cross round my neck, and if ever I broke those terms, even for a moment, my life was his who cared to take it, without blame or penalty. And I could never return.' Another fire, of banished love, ruined ambition, rejected service, flamed through the broken accents for a moment, and died of despair.

'Yet if this sentence was never made public,' said Hugh, seizing upon one thing still unexplained, 'how did Luc Meverel ever come to know of it and follow you?'

'Do I know?' The voice was flat and drear, worn out with exhaustion. 'All I know is that I set out from Winchester, and where the roads joined, near Newbury, this man stood and waited for me, and fell in beside me, and every step of my way on this journey he has gone on my heels like a demon, and waited for me to play false to my sentence—for there was no point of it he did not know!—to take my life without guilt, without a qualm, as so he might. He trod after me wherever I trod, he never let me from his sight, he made no secret of his wants, he tempted me to go aside, to put on shoes, to lay by the cross—and sirs, it was deathly heavy! Matthew, he called himself ... Luc, you say he is? You know him? I never knew ... He said I had killed his lord, whom he loved, and he would follow me to Bangor, to Caergybi, even to Dublin if ever I got aboard ship without putting off the cross or putting on shoes. But he would have me in the end. He had what he lusted for—why did he turn away and spare?' The last words ached with his uncomprehending wonder.

'He did not find you worth the killing,' said Cadfael, as gently and mercifully as he could, but honestly. 'Now he goes in anguish and shame because he spent so much time on you that might have been better spent. It is a matter of values. Study to learn what is worth and what is not, and you may come to understand him.'

'I am a dead man while I live,' said Ciaran, writhing, 'without master, without friends, without a cause . . .'

'All three you may find, if you seek. Go where you were sent, bear what you were condemned to bear, and look for the meaning,' said Cadfael. 'For so must we all.'

He turned away with a sigh. No way of knowing how much good words might do, or the lessons of life, no telling whether any trace of compunction moved in Ciaran's bludgeoned mind, or whether all his feeling was still for himself. Cadfael felt himself suddenly very tired. He looked at Hugh with a somewhat lopsided smile. 'I wish I were home. What now, Hugh? Can we go?'

Hugh stood looking down with a frown at the confessed murderer, sunken in the grass like a broken-backed serpent, submissive, tear-stained, nursing minor injuries. A piteous spectacle, though pity might be misplaced. Yet he was, after all, no more than twenty-five or so years old, able-bodied, well-clothed, strong, his continued journey might be painful and arduous, but it was not beyond his powers, and he had his bishop's ring still, effective wherever law held. These three footpads now tethered fast and under guard would trouble his going no more. Ciaran would surely reach his journey's end safely, however long it might take him. Not the journey's end of his false story, a blessed death in Aberdaron and burial among the saints of Ynys Ennli, but a return to his native place, and a life beginning afresh. He might even be changed. He might well adhere to his hard terms all the way to Caergybi, where Irish ships plied, even as far as Dublin, even to his ransomed life's end. How can you tell?

'Make your own way from here,' said Hugh, 'as well as you may. You need fear nothing now from footpads here, and the border is not far. What you have to fear from God, take up with God.'

He turned his back, with so decisive a movement that his men recognised the sign that all was over, and stirred willingly about the captives and the horses.

'And those two?' asked Hugh. 'Had I not better leave a man behind on the track there, with a spare horse for Luc? He followed his quarry afoot, but no need for him to foot it

248

back. Or ought I to send men after them?'

'No need for that,' said Cadfael with certainty. 'Olivier will manage all. They'll come home together.'

He had no qualms at all, he was beginning to relax into the warmth of content. The evil he had dreaded had been averted, however narrowly, at whatever cost. Olivier would find his stray, bear with him, follow if he tried to avoid, wrung and ravaged as he was, with the sole obsessive purpose of his life for so long ripped away from him, and within him only the aching emptiness where that consuming passion had been. Into that barren void Olivier would win his way, and warm the ravished heart to make it habitable for another love. There was the most comforting of messages to bring from Juliana Bossard, the promise regained of a home and a welcome. There was a future. How had Matthew-Luc seen his future when he emptied his purse of the last coin at the abbey, before taking up the pursuit of his enemy? Surely he had been contemplating the end of the person he had hitherto been, a total ending, beyond which he could not see. Now he was young again, there was a life before him, it needed only a little time to make him whole again.

Olivier would bring him back to the abbey, when the worst desolation was over. For Olivier had promised that he would not leave without spending some time leisurely with

Cadfael, and upon Olivier's promise the heart could rest secure.

As for the other ... Cadfael looked back from the saddle, after they had mounted, and saw the last of Ciaran, still on his knees under the tree, where they had left him. His face was turned to them, but his eyes seemed to be closed, and his hands were wrung tightly together before his breast. He might have been praying, he might have been simply experiencing with every particle of his flesh the life that had been left to him. When we are all gone, thought Cadfael, he will fall asleep there where he lies, he can do no other, for he is far gone in something beyond exhaustion. Where he falls asleep, there he will have died. But when he awakes, I trust he may understand that he has been born again.

The slower cortège that would bring the prisoners into the town began to assemble, making the tethering thongs secure, and the torch-bearers crossed the clearing to mount, withdrawing their yellow light from the kneeling figure, so that Ciaran vanished gradually, as though he had been absorbed into the bole of the beech-tree.

Hugh led the way out to the track, and turned homeward. 'Oh, Hugh, I grow old!' said Cadfael, hugely yawning. 'I want my bed.'

CHAPTER FIFTEEN

It was past midnight when they rode in at the gatehouse, into a great court awash with moonlight, and heard the chanting of Matins within the church. They had made no haste on the way home, and said very little, content to ride companionably together as sometimes before, through summer night or winter day. It would be another hour or more yet before Hugh's officers got their prisoners back to Shrewsbury Castle, since they must keep a foot-pace, but before morning Simeon Poer and his henchmen would be safe in hold, under lock and key.

'I'll wait with you until Lauds is over,' said Hugh, as they dismounted at the gatehouse. 'Father Abbot will want to know how we've sped. Though I hope he won't require the whole tale from us tonight.'

'Come down with me to the stables, then,' said Cadfael, 'and I'll see this fellow unsaddled and tended, while they're still within. I was always taught to care for my beast before seeking my own rest. You never lose the habit.'

In the stable-yard the moonlight was all the light they needed. The quietness of midnight and the stillness of the air carried every note of the office to them softly and clearly. Cadfael unsaddled his horse and saw him settled and

251

provided in his stall, with a light rug against any possible chill, rites he seldom had occasion to perform now. They brought back memories of other mounts and other journeys, and battlefields less happily resolved than the small but desperate skirmish just lost and won.

Hugh stood watching with his back turned to the great court, but his head tilted to follow the chant. Yet it was not any sound of an approaching step that made him look round suddenly, but the slender shadow that stole along the moonlit cobbles beside his feet. And there hesitant in the gateway of the yard stood Melangell, startled and startling, haloed in that pallid sheen.

'Child,' said Cadfael, concerned, 'what are you doing out of your bed at this hour?'

'How could I rest?' she said, but not as one complaining. 'No one misses me, they are all sleeping.' She stood very still and straight, as if she had spent all the hours since he had left her in earnest endeavour to put away for ever any memories he might have of the tear-stained, despairing girl who had sought solitude in his workshop. The great sheaf of her hair was braided and pinned up on her head, her gown was trim, and her face resolutely calm as she asked, 'Did you find him?'

A girl he had left her, a woman he came back to her. 'Yes,' said Cadfael, 'we found them both. There has nothing ill happened to

252

either. The two of them have parted. Ciaran goes on his way alone.'

'And Matthew?' she asked steadily.

'Matthew is with a good friend, and will come to no harm. We two have outridden them, but they will come.' She would have to learn to call him by another name now, but let the man himself tell her that. Nor would the future be altogether easy, for her or for Luc Meverel, two human creatures who might never have been brought within hail of each other but for freakish circumstance. Unless Saint Winifred had had a hand in that, too? On this night Cadfael could believe it, and trust her to bring all to a good end. 'He will come back,' said Cadfael, meeting her candid eyes, that bore no trace of tears now. 'You need not fear. But he has suffered a great turmoil of the mind, and he'll need all your patience and wisdom. Ask him nothing. When the time is right he will tell you everything. Reproach him with nothing—'

'God forbid,' she said, 'that I should ever reproach him. It was I who failed him.'

'No, how could you know? But when he comes, wonder at nothing. Be like one who is thirsty and drinks. And so will he.'

She had turned a little towards him, and the moonlight blanched wonderfully over her face, as if a lamp within her had been newly lighted. 'I will wait,' she said.

'Better go to your bed and sleep, the waiting

253

may be longer than you think, he has been wrung. But he will come.'

But at that she shook her head. 'I'll watch till he comes,' she said, and suddenly smiled at them, pale and lustrous as pearl, and turned and went away swiftly and silently towards the cloister.

'That is the girl you spoke of?' asked Hugh, looking after her with somewhat frowning interest. 'The lame boy's sister? The girl that young man fancies?'

'That is she,' said Cadfael, and closed the half-door of the stall.

'The weaver-woman's niece?'

'That, too. Dowerless and from common stock,' said Cadfael, understanding but untroubled. 'Yes, true! I'm from common stock myself. I doubt if a young fellow who has been torn apart and remade as Luc has tonight will care much about such little things. Though I grant you others may! I hope the lady Juliana has no plans yet for marrying him off to some heiress from a neighbour manor, for I fancy things have gone so far now with these two that she'll be forced to abandon her plans. A manor or a craft—if you take pride in them, and run them well, where's the difference?'

'Your common stock,' said Hugh heartily, 'gave growth to a most uncommon shoot! And I wouldn't say but that young thing would grace a hall better than many a highbred dame I've seen. But listen, they're ending. We'd best

254

present ourselves.'

*   *   *

Abbot Radulfus came from Matins and Lauds with his usual imperturbable stride, and found them waiting for him as he left the cloister. This day of miracles had produced a fittingly glorious night, incredibly lofty and deep, coruscating with stars, washed white with moonlight. Coming from the dimness within, this exuberance of light showed him clearly both the serenity and the weariness on the two faces that confronted him.

'You are back!' he said, and looked beyond them. 'But not all! Messire de Bretagne—you said he had gone by a wrong way. He has not returned here. You have not encountered him?'

'Yes, Father, we have,' said Hugh. 'All is well with him, and he has found the young man he was seeking. They will return here, all in good time.'

'And the evil you feared, Brother Cadfael? You spoke of another death . . .'

'Father,' said Cadfael, 'no harm has come tonight to any but the masterless men who escaped into the forest there. They are now safe in hold, and on their way under guard to the castle. The death I dreaded has been averted, no threat remains in that quarter to any man. I said, if the two young men could be

255

overtaken, the better surely for one, and perhaps for both. Father, they were overtaken in time, and better for both it surely must be.'

'Yet there remains,' said Radulfus, pondering, 'the print of blood, which both you and I have seen. You said—you will recall—that, yes, we have entertained a murderer among us. Do you still say so?'

'Yes, Father. Yet not as you suppose. When Olivier de Bretagne and Luc Meverel return, then all can be made plain, for as yet,' said Cadfael, 'there are still certain things we do not know. But we do know,' he said firmly, 'that what has passed this night is the best for which we could have prayed, and we have good need to give thanks for it.'

'So all is well?'

'All is very well, Father.'

'Then the rest may wait for morning. You need rest. But will you not come in with me and take some food and wine, before you sleep?'

'My wife,' said Hugh, gracefully evading, 'will be in some anxiety for me. You are kind, Father, but I would not have her fret longer than she need.'

The abbot eyed them both, and did not press them.

'And God bless you for that!' sighed Cadfael, toiling up the slight slope of the court towards the dortoir stair and the gatehouse where Hugh had hitched his horse. 'For I'm

256

asleep on my feet, and even a good wine could not revive me.'

* * *

The moonlight was gone, and there was as yet no sunlight, when Olivier de Bretagne and Luc Meverel rode slowly in at the abbey gatehouse. How far they had wandered in the deep night neither of them knew very clearly, for this was strange country to both. Even when overtaken, and addressed with careful gentleness, Luc had still gone forward blindly, hands hanging slack at his sides or vaguely parting the bushes, saying nothing, hearing nothing, unless some core of feeling within him was aware of this calm, relentless pursuit by a tolerant, incurious kindness, and distantly wondered at it. When he had dropped at last and lain down in the lush grass of a meadow at the edge of the forest, Olivier had tethered his horse a little apart and lain down beside him, not too close, yet so close that the mute man knew he was there, waiting without impatience. Past midnight Luc had fallen asleep. It was his greatest need. He was a man ravished and emptied of every impulse that had held him alive for the past two months, a dead man still walking and unable quite to die. Sleep was his ransom. Then he could truly die to this waste of loss and bitterness, the awful need that had driven him, the corrosive grief that had eaten

257

his heart out for his lord, who had died in his arms, on his shoulder, on his heart. The bloodstain that would not wash out, no matter how he laboured over it, was his witness. He had kept it to keep the fire of his hatred white-hot. Now in sleep he was delivered from all.

And he had awakened in the first mysterious pre-dawn stirring of the earliest summer birds, beginning to call tentatively into the silence, to open his eyes upon a face bending over him, a face he did not know, but remotely desired to know, for it was vivid, friendly and calm, waiting courteously on his will.

'Did I kill him?' Luc had asked, somehow aware that the man who bore this face would know the answer.

'No,' said a voice clear, serene and low. 'There was no need. But he's dead to you. You can forget him.'

He did not understand that, but he accepted it. He sat up in the cool, ripe grass, and his senses began to stir again, and record distantly that the earth smelled sweet, and there were paling stars in the sky over him, caught like stray sparks in the branches of the trees. He stared intently into Olivier's face, and Olivier looked back at him with a slight, serene smile, and was silent.

'Do I know you?' asked Luc wonderingly.

'No. But you will. My name is Olivier de Bretagne, and I serve Laurence d'Angers, just

258

as your lord did. I knew Rainald Bossard well, he was my friend, we came from the Holy Land together in Laurence's train. And I am sent with a message to Luc Meverel, and that, I am sure, is your name.'

'A message to me?' Luc shook his head.

'From your cousin and lady, Juliana Bossard. And the message is that she begs you to come home, for she needs you, and there is no one who can take your place.'

He was slow to believe, still numbed and hollow within; but there was no impulsion for him to go anywhere or do anything now of his own will, and he yielded indifferently to Olivier's promptings. 'Now we should be getting back to the abbey,' said Olivier practically, and rose, and Luc responded, and rose with him. 'You take the horse, and I'll walk,' said Olivier, and Luc did as he was bidden. It was like nursing a simpleton gently along the way he must go, and holding him by the hand at every step.

They found their way back at last to the old track, and there were the two horses Hugh had left behind for them, and the groom fast asleep in the grass beside them. Olivier took back his own horse, and Luc mounted the fresh one, with the lightness and ease of custom, his body's instincts at least reawakening. The yawning groom led the way, knowing the path well. Not until they were halfway back towards the Meole brook and the narrow bridge to the highroad did Luc say a word of his own volition.

'You say she wants me to come back,' he said abruptly, with quickening pain and hope in his voice. 'Is it true? I left her without a word, but what else could I do? What can she think of me now?'

'Why, that you had your reasons for leaving her, as she has hers for wanting you back. Half the length of England I have been asking after you, at her entreaty. What more do you need?'

'I never thought to return,' said Luc, staring back down that long, long road in wonder and doubt.

No, not even to Shrewsbury, much less to his home in the south. Yet here he was, in the cool, soft morning twilight well before Prime, riding beside this young stranger over the wooden bridge that crossed the Meole brook, instead of wading through the shrunken stream to the pease-fields, the way by which he had left the enclave. Round to the highroad, past the mill and the pond, and in at the gatehouse to the great court. There they lighted down, and the groom took himself and his two horses briskly away again towards the town.

Luc stood gazing about him dully, still clouded by the unfamiliarity of everything he beheld, as if his senses were still dazed and clumsy with the effort of coming back to life. At this hour the court was empty. No, not

260

quite empty. There was someone sitting on the stone steps that climbed to the door of the guest-hall, sitting there alone and quite composedly, with her face turned towards the gate, and as he watched she rose and came down the wide steps, and walked towards him with a swift, light step. Then he knew her for Melangell.

In her at least there was nothing unfamiliar. The sight of her brought back colour and form and reality into the very stones of the wall at her back, and the cobbles under her feet. The elusive grey between-light could not blur the outlines of head and hand, or dim the brightness of her hair. Life came flooding back into Luc with a shock of pain, as feeling returns after a numbing wound. She came towards him with hands a little extended and face raised, and the faintest and most anxious of smiles on her lips and in her eyes. Then, as she hesitated for the first time, a few paces from him, he saw the dark stain of the bruise that marred her cheek.

It was the bruise that shattered him. He shook from head to heels in a great convulsion of shame and grief, and blundered forward blindly into her arms, which reached gladly to receive him. On his knees, with his arms wound about her and his face buried in her breast, he burst into a storm of tears, as spontaneous and as healing as Saint Winifred's own miraculous spring.

He was in perfect command of voice and face when they met after chapter in the abbot's parlour, abbot, prior, Brother Cadfael, Hugh Beringar, Olivier and Luc, to set right in all its details the account of Rainald Bossard's death, and all that had followed from it.

'Unwittingly I deceived you, Father,' said Cadfael, harking back to the interview which had sent him forth in such haste. 'When you asked if we had entertained a murderer unawares, I answered truly that I did think so, but that we might yet have time to prevent a second death. I never realised until afterwards how you might interpret that, seeing we had just found the blood-stained shirt. But, see, the man who struck the blow might be spattered as to sleeve or collar, but he would not be marked by this great blot that covered breast and shoulder over the heart. No, that was rather the sign of one who had held a wounded man, a man wounded to death, in his arms as he died. Nor would the slayer, if his clothing was blood-stained, have kept and carried it with him, but burned or buried it, or somehow rid himself of it. But this shirt, though washed most carefully, still bore the outline of the stain clear to be seen, and it was carried as a sacred relic is carried, perhaps as a pledge to exact vengeance. So I knew that this same Luc whom we knew as Matthew, and in whose scrip the talisman was found, was not the murderer. But when I recalled all the words I had heard those two young men speak, and all the evidence of devoted attendance, the one on the other, then suddenly I saw that pairing in the utterly opposed way, as a pursuit. And I feared it must be to the death.'

The abbot looked at Luc, and asked simply: 'Is that a true reading?'

'Father, it is.' Luc set forth with deliberation the progress of his own obsession, as though he discovered it and understood it only in speaking. 'I was with my lord that night, close to the Old Minster it was, when four or five set on the clerk, and my lord ran, and we with him, to beat them off. And then they fled, but one turned back and struck. I saw it done, and it was done of intent! I had my lord in my arms—he had been good to me, and I loved him,' said Luc with grimly measured moderation and burning eyes as he remembered. 'He was dead in a mere moment, in the twinkling of an eye ... And I had seen where the murderer fled, into the passage by the chapter house. I went after him, and I heard their voices in the sacristy—Bishop Henry had come from the chapter house after the council ended for the night, and there Ciaran had found him and fell on his knees to him, blurting out all. I lay in hiding, and heard every word. I think he even hoped for praise,'

263

said Luc with bitter deliberation.

'Is it possible?' wondered Prior Robert, shocked to the heart. 'Bishop Henry could not for one moment connive at or condone an act so evil.'

'No, he did not condone. But neither would he deliver over one of his own intimate servants as a murderer. To do him justice,' said Luc, but with plain distaste, 'his concern was not to cause further anger and quarrelling, but to put away and smooth over everything that threatened the empress's fortunes and the peace he was trying to make. But condone murder—no, that he would not. Therefore I overheard the sentence he laid upon Ciaran—though then I did not know who he was, nor that Ciaran was his name. He banished him back to his Dublin home, for ever, and condemned him to go every step of the way to Bangor and to the ship at Caergybi barefoot, and carrying that heavy cross. And if ever he put on shoes or laid by the cross from round his neck, then his forfeit life was no longer spared, but might be taken by whoever willed, without sin or penalty. But see,' said Luc, merciless in judgement, 'how he cheated! For not only did he give his creature the ring that would ensure him the protection of the church to Bangor, but also, mark, not one word was ever made public of this guilt or this sentence, so how was that forfeit life in danger? No one was to know of it but they two, if God had not

264

prevented and brought there a witness to hear the sentence and take upon himself the vengeance due.'

'As you did,' said the abbot, and his voice was even and calm, avoiding judgement.

'As I did, Father. For as Ciaran swore to keep the terms laid down on pain of death, so did I swear an oath as solemn to follow him the length of the land, and if ever he broke his terms for a moment, to have his life as payment for my lord.'

'And how,' asked Radulfus in the same mild tone, 'did you know what man you were thus to hunt to his death? For you say you did not see his face clearly or know his name then.'

'I knew the way he was bound to go, and the day of his setting out. I waited by the roadside for one walking north, barefoot—and one not used to going barefoot, but very well shod,' said Luc with a brief, wry smile. 'I saw the cross at his neck. I fell in at his side, and I told him, not who I was, but what. I took another name, so that no failure nor shame of mine should ever cast a shadow on my lady or her house. One Evangelist in exchange for another! Step for step with him I went all this way, here to this place, and never let him from my sight and reach, night or day, and never let him forget that I meant to be his death. He could not ask help to rid himself of me, since I could then as easily strip him of his pilgrim holiness and show what he really was. And I

265

could not denounce him—partly for fear of Bishop Henry, partly because neither did I want more feuding between factions—my feud was between two men!—but chiefly because he was mine, mine, and I would not let any other vengeance or danger reach him. So we kept together, he trying to elude me—but he was court-bred and tender and crippled by the miles—and I holding fast to him, and waiting.'

He looked up suddenly and caught the abbot's compassionate but calm eyes upon him, and his own eyes were wide, dark and clear. 'It is not beautiful, I know. Neither was murder beautiful. And this blotch was only mine—my lord went to his grave immaculate, defending one opposed to him.'

It was Olivier, silent until now, who said softly: *'And so did you!'*

* * *

The grave, thought Cadfael at the height of the Mass, had closed firmly to deny Luc entrance, but that arm outstretched between his enemy and the knives of three assailants must never be forgotten. Hell had also shut its mouth and refused to devour him. He was young, clean, alive again after a kind of death. Yes, Olivier had uttered truth. His own life ventured, his enemy's life defended, what was there between Luc and his lord but the accident, the vain and random accident, of the death itself?

He recalled also, when he was most diligent in prayer, that these few days while Saint Winifred was manifesting her virtue in disentangling the troubled lives of some half-dozen people in Shrewsbury, were also the vital days when the fates of Englishmen in general were being determined, perhaps with less compassion and wisdom. For by this time the date of the empress's coronation might well be settled, the crown even now placed upon her head. No doubt God and the saints had that consideration in mind, too.

*   *   *

Matthew-Luc came once again to ask audience of the abbot, a little before Vespers. Radulfus had him admitted without question, and sat with him alone, divining his present need.

'Father, will you hear me my confession? For I need absolution from the vow I could not keep. And I do earnestly desire to be clean of the past before I undertake the future.'

'It is a right and a wise desire,' said Radulfus. 'One thing tell me—are you asking absolution for failing to fulfil the oath you swore?'

Luc, already on his knees, raised his head for a moment from the abbot's knee, and showed a face open and clear. 'No, Father, but for ever swearing such an oath. Even grief has its arrogance.'

'Then you have learned, my son, that vengeance belongs only to God?'

'More than that, Father,' said Luc. 'I have learned that in God's hands vengeance is safe. However long delayed, however strangely manifested, the reckoning is sure.'

When it was done, when he had raked out of his heart, with measured voice and long pauses for thought, every drifted grain of rancour and bitterness and impatience that fretted him, and received absolution, he rose with a great sigh, and raised a bright and resolute face.

'Now, Father, if I may pray of you one more grace, let me have one of your priests to join me to a wife before I go from here. Here, where I am made clean and new, I would have love and life begin together.'

CHAPTER SIXTEEN

On the next morning, which was the twenty-fourth day of June, the general bustle of departure began. There was packing of belongings, buying and parcelling of food and drink for the journey, and much leave-taking from friends newly made, and arranging of company for the road. No doubt the saint would have due regard for her own reputation, and keep the June sun shining until all her devotees were safely home, and with a wonderful tale to tell. Most of them knew only half the wonder, but even that was wonder enough.

Among the early departures went Brother Adam of Reading, in no great hurry along the way, for today he would go no farther than Reading's daughter-house of Leominster, where there would be letters waiting for him to carry home to his abbot. He set out with a pouch well filled with seeds of species his garden did not yet possess, and a scholarly mind still pondering the miraculous healing he had witnessed from every theological angle, in order to be able to expound its full significance when he reached his own monastery. It had been a most instructive and enlightening festival.

'I'd meant to start for home today, too,' said Mistress Weaver to her cronies Mistress Glover and the apothecary's widow, with whom she had formed a strong matronly alliance during these memorable days, 'but now there's such work doing, I hardly know whether I'm waking or sleeping, and I must stay over yet a night or two. Who'd ever have thought what would come of it, when I told my lad we ought to come and make our prayers here to the good saint, and have faith that she'd be listening? Now it seems I'm to lose the both of them, my poor sister's chicks; for

Rhun, God bless him, is set on staying here and taking the cowl, for he says he won't ever leave the blessed girl who healed him. And truly I don't wonder at it, and won't stand in his way, for he's too good for this wicked world outside, so he is! And now comes young Matthew—no, but it seems we must call him Luc, now, and he's well-born, if from a poor landless branch, and will come in for a manor or two in time, by his good kinswoman's taking him in . . .'

'Well, and so did you take the boy and girl in,' pointed out the apothecary's widow warmly, 'and gave them a roof and a living. There's good sound justice there.'

'Well, so Matthew, I mean Luc, he comes to me and asks for my girl for his wife, last night it was, and when I answered honestly, for honest I am and always will be, that my Melangell has but a meagre dowry, though the best I can give her I will, what says he? That as at this moment he himself has not one penny to his name in this world, but must go debtor to the young lord's charity that came to find him, and as for the future, if fortune favours him he'll be thankful, and if not, he has hands and a will, and can make a way for two to live. Provided the other is my girl, he says, for there's none other for him. So what can I say but God bless them both, and stay to see them wedded?'

'It's a woman's duty,' said Mistress Glover

heartily, 'to make sure all's done properly, when she hands over a young girl to a husband. But sure, you'll miss the two of them.'

'So I will,' agreed Dame Alice, shedding a few tears rather of pride and joy than of grief, at the advancement to semi-sainthood and promising matrimony of the charges who had cost her dear enough, and could now be blessed and sped on their respective and respectable ways with a quiet mind. 'So I will! But to see them both set up where they would be ... And good children both, that will take pains for me when I come to need, as I have for them.'

'And they're to marry here, tomorrow?' asked the apothecary's widow, visibly considering putting off her own departure for another day.

'They are indeed, before Mass in the morning. So it seems I'll have none to take home but my sole self,' said Dame Alice, dropping another proud tear or two, and wearing her reflected glory with admirable grace, 'when I take to the road again. But the day after tomorrow there's a sturdy company leaving southward, and with them I'll go.'

'And duty well done, my dear soul,' said Mistress Glover, embracing her friend in a massive arm, 'duty very well done!'

*   *   *

They were married in the privacy of the Lady Chapel, by Brother Paul, who was not only master of the novices, but the chief of their confessors, too, and already had Rhun under his care and instruction, and felt a fatherly interest in him, which the boy's affection very readily extended to embrace the sister. No one else was present but the family and their witnesses, and the bridal pair wore no festal garments, for they had none. Luc was in the serviceable brown cotte and hose he had slept in, out in the fields, and the same crumpled shirt, though newly washed and smoothed. Melangell was neat and modest in her homespun, proudly balancing her coronal of braided, deep-gold hair. They were pale as lilies, bright as stars, and solemn as the grave.

*   *   *

After high and moving events, daily life must still go on. Cadfael went to his work that afternoon well content. With the meadow grasses in ripe seed and the harvest imminent he had preparations to make for two seasonal ailments which could be relied upon to recur every year. There were some who suffered with eruptions on their hands when working in the harvest, and others who took to sneezing and wheezing, with running eyes, and needed lotions to help them.

He was busy bruising fresh leaves of dock and mandrake in a mortar for a soothing ointment, when he heard light, long-striding steps approaching along the gravel of the path, and then half of the sunlight from the wide-open door was cut off, as someone hesitated in the doorway. He turned with the mortar hugged to his chest, and the green-stained wooden pestle arrested in his hand, and there stood Olivier, dipping his tall head to evade the hanging bunches of herbs, and asking, in the mellow, confident voice of one assured of the answer, 'May I come in?'

He was in already, smiling, staring about him with a boy's candid curiosity, for he had never been here before. 'I've been a truant, I know, but with two days to wait before Luc's marriage I thought best to get on with my errand to the sheriff of Stafford, being so close, and then come back here. I was back, as I said I'd be, in time to see them wedded. I thought you would have been there.'

'So I would, but I was called out to Saint Giles. Some poor soul of a beggar stumbled in there overnight covered with sores, they were afraid of a contagion, but it's no such matter. If he'd had treatment earlier it would have been an easy matter to cure him, but a week or so resting in the hospital will do him no harm. Our pair of youngsters here had no need of me. I'm a part of what's over and done with for them, you're a part of what's beginning.'

'Melangell told me where I should find you, however, you were missed. And here I am.'

'And as welcome as the day,' said Cadfael, laying his mortar aside. Long, shapely hands gripped both his hands heartily, and Olivier stooped his olive cheek for the greeting kiss, as simply as for the parting kiss when they had separated at Bromfield. 'Come, sit, let me offer you wine—my own making. You knew, then, that those two would marry?'

'I saw them meet, when I brought him back here. Small doubt how it would end. Afterwards he told me his intent. When two are agreed, and know their own minds,' said Olivier blithely, 'everything else will give way. I shall see them both properly provided for the journey home, since I must go by a more roundabout way.'

When two are agreed, and know their own minds! Cadfael remembered confidences now a year and a half past. He poured wine carefully, his hand being a shade less steady than usual, and sat down beside his visitor, the young, wide shoulder firm and vital against his elderly and stiff one, the clear, elegant profile close, and a pleasure to his eyes. 'Tell me,' he said, 'about Ermina,' and was sure of the answer even before Olivier turned on him his sudden blinding smile.

'If I had known my travels would bring me to you, I should have had so many messages to bring you, from both of them. From Yves—

274

and from my wife!'

'Aaaah!' breathed Cadfael, on a deep, delighted sigh. 'So, as I thought, as I hoped! You have made good, then, what you told me, that they would acknowledge your worth and give her to you.' Two, there, who had indeed known their own minds, and been invincibly agreed! 'When was this match made?'

'This Christmas past, in Gloucester. She is there now, so is the boy. He is Laurence's heir—just fifteen now. He wanted to come to Winchester with us, but Laurence wouldn't let him be put in peril. They are safe, I thank God. If ever this chaos is ended,' said Olivier very solemnly, 'I will bring her to you, or you to her. She does not forget you.'

'Nor I her, nor I her! Nor the boy. He rode with me twice, asleep in my arms, I still recall the warmth and the shape and the weight of him. A good boy as ever stepped!'

'He'd be a load for you now,' said Olivier, laughing. 'This year past, he's shot up like a weed, he'll be taller than you.'

'Ah, well; I'm beginning to shrink like a spent weed. And you are happy?' asked Cadfael, thirsting for more blessedness even than he already had. 'You and she both?'

'Beyond what I know how to express,' said Olivier no less gravely. 'How glad I am to have seen you again, and been able to tell you so! Do you remember the last time? When I waited with you in Bromfield to take Ermina

275

and Yves home? And you drew me maps on the floor to show me the ways?'

There is a point at which joy is only just bearable. Cadfael got up to refill the wine-cups, and turn his face away for a moment from a brightness almost too bright. 'Ah, now, if this is to be a contest in "do-you-remembers" we shall be at it until Vespers, for not one detail of that time have I forgotten. So let's have this flask here within reach, and settle down to it in comfort.'

*   *   *

But there was an hour and more left before Vespers when Hugh put an abrupt end to remembering. He came in haste, with a face blazingly alert, and full of news. Even so he was slow to speak, not wishing to exult openly in what must be only shock and dismay to Olivier.

'There's news. A courier rode in from Warwick just now, they're passing the word north by stages as fast as horse can go.' They were both on their feet by then, intent upon his face, and waiting for good or evil, for he contained it well. A good face for keeping secrets, and under strong control now out of courteous consideration. 'I fear,' he said, 'it will not come as gratefully to you, Olivier, as I own it does to me.'

'From the south . . .' said Olivier, braced

276

and still. 'From London? The empress?'

'Yes, from London. All is overturned in a day. There'll be no coronation. Yesterday as they sat at dinner in Westminster, the Londoners suddenly rang the tocsin—all the city bells. The entire town came out in arms, and marched on Westminster. They're fled, Olivier, she and all her court, fled in the clothes they wore and with very little else, and the city men have plundered the palace and driven out even the last hangers-on. She never made move to win them, nothing but threats and reproaches and demands for money ever since she entered. She's let the crown slip through her fingers for want of a few soft words and a queen's courtesy. For your part,' said Hugh, with real compunction, 'I'm sorry! For mine, I find it a great deliverance.'

'With that I find no fault,' said Olivier simply. 'Why should you not be glad? But she . . . she's safe? They have not taken her?'

'No, according to the messenger she's safely away, with Robert of Gloucester and a few others as loyal, but the rest, it seems, scattered and made off for their own lands, where they'd feel safe. That's the word as he brought it, barely a day old. The city of London was being pressed hard from the south,' said Hugh, somewhat softening the load of folly that lay upon the empress's own shoulders, 'with King Stephen's queen harrying their borders. To get relief their only way was to drive the empress out and let the queen in, and their hearts were on her side, no question, of the two they'd liefer have her.'

'I knew,' said Olivier, 'she was not wise—the Empress Maud. I knew she could not forget grudges, no matter how sorely she needed to close her eyes to them. I have seen her strip a man's dignity from him when he came submissive, offering support ... Better at making enemies than friends. All the more she needs,' he said, 'the few she has. Where is she gone? Did your messenger know?'

'Westward for Oxford. And they'll reach it safely. The Londoners won't follow so far, their part was only to drive her out.'

'And the bishop? Is he gone with her?' The entire enterprise had rested upon the efforts of Henry of Blois, and he had done his best for her, not entirely creditably but understandably and at considerable cost, and his best she herself had undone. Stephen was a prisoner in Bristol, but Stephen was still crowned and anointed king of England. No wonder Hugh's eyes shone.

'Of the bishop I know nothing as yet. But he'll surely join her in Oxford. Unless . . .'

'Unless he changes sides again,' Olivier ended for him, and laughed. 'It seems I shall have to leave you in more haste than I expected,' he said with regret. 'One fortune rises, another falls. No sense in quarrelling with the lot.'

'What will you do?' asked Hugh, watching him steadily. 'You know, I think, that whatever you may ask of us here, is yours, and the choice is yours. Your horses are fresh. Your men will not yet have heard the news, they'll be waiting on your word. If you need stores for a journey, take whatever you will. Or if you choose to stay . . .'

Olivier shook his blue-black head, and the clasping curves of glossy hair danced on his cheeks. 'I must go. Not north, where I was sent. What use in that, now? South for Oxford. Whatever she may be else, she is my liege lord's liege lady, where she is he will be, and where he is, I go.'

They eyed each other silently for a moment, and Hugh said softly, quoting remembered words: 'To tell you truth, now I've met you I expected nothing less.'

'I'll go and rouse my men, and we'll get to horse. You'll follow to your house, before I go? I must take leave of Lady Beringar.'

'I'll follow you,' said Hugh.

Olivier turned to Brother Cadfael without a word but with the brief golden flash of a smile breaking through his roused gravity for an instant, and again vanishing. 'Brother . . . remember me in your prayers!' He stooped his smooth cheek yet again in farewell, and as the elder's kiss was given he embraced Cadfael vehemently, with impulsive grace. 'Until a better time!'

'God go with you!' said Cadfael.

And he was gone, striding rapidly along the gravel path, breaking into a light run, in no way disheartened or down, a match for disaster or for triumph. At the corner of the box hedge he turned in flight to look back, and waved a hand before he vanished.

'I wish to God,' said Hugh, gazing after him, 'he was of our party! There's an odd thing, Cadfael! Will you believe, just then, when he looked round, I thought I saw something of you about him. The set of the head, something . . .'

Cadfael, too, was gazing out from the open doorway to where the last sheen of blue had flashed from the burnished hair, and the last echo of the light foot on the gravel died into silence. 'Oh, no,' he said absently, 'he is altogether the image of his mother.'

An unguarded utterance. Unguarded from absence of mind, or design?

The following silence did not trouble him, he continued to gaze, shaking his head gently over the lingering vision, which would stay with him through all his remaining years, and might even, by the grace of God and the saints, be made flesh for him yet a third time. Far beyond his deserts, but miracles are neither weighed nor measured, but as uncalculated as the lightnings.

'I recall,' said Hugh with careful deliberation, perceiving that he was permitted to speculate, and had heard only what he was meant to hear, 'I do recall that he spoke of one for whose sake he held the Benedictine order in reverence ... one who had used him like a son ...'

Cadfael stirred, and looked round at him, smiling as he met his friend's fixed and thoughtful eyes. 'I always meant to tell you, some day,' he said tranquilly, 'what he does not know, and never will from me. He *is* my son.'